ANGELS BENEATH THE SURFACE

D1446995

angels beneath the surface

A SELECTION OF CONTEMPORARY SLOVENE FICTION

Edited by

MITJA ČANDER

with

TOM PRIESTLY

North Atlantic Books
Berkeley, California

Scala House Press
Seattle, Washington

Published by

North Atlantic Books   Scala House Press
P.O. Box 12327   P. O. Box 4518
Berkeley, California 94712   Seattle, Washington 98194

Printed in the United States of America
Cover image © Denise Roup/iStockphoto.com
Cover and book design © Ayelet Maida, A/M Studios.

This anthology was published in partnership with Beletrina, an imprint of Študentska založba (Academic Press) in Ljubljana, Slovenia. Our thanks to Gorazd Trušnovec at Beletrina.

This publication was supported in part by a grant from the Trubar Foundation, a joint venture of Slovene Writers' Association, Slovenian PEN, and the Center for Slovenian Literature. The Trubar Foundation is located in Ljubljana, Slovenia.

Many of these stories appeared in slightly different forms in *The Key Witnesses: The Younger Slovene Prose at the Turn of the Millennia* (Slovene Writers' Association, 2003). Our thanks to the Slovene Writers' Association for their help.

A version of "The Fall of the House of Pirnat" by Maya Novak appeared in AGNI 63 and on AGNI Online.

Angels Beneath the Surface: A Selection of Contemporary Slovene Fiction is sponsored by the Society for the Study of Native Arts and Sciences, a nonprofit educational corporation whose goals are to develop an educational and cross-cultural perspective linking various scientific, social, and artistic fields; to nurture a holistic view of arts, sciences, humanities, and healing; and to publish and distribute literature on the relationship of mind, body, and nature.

North Atlantic Books' publications are available through most bookstores. For further information, call 800-733-3000 or visit our website at www.northatlantic books.com.

Library of Congress Cataloging-in-Publication Data
Angels beneath the surface : a selection of contemporary Slovene fiction / edited by Tom Priestly ; introduction by Mitja Čander and Aleš Šteger
    p. cm.
  ISBN 978-1-55643-703-8
  1. Slovenian prose literature—Translations into English. 2. Slovenian literature—Translations into English. I. Priestly, Tom M. S. II. Čander, Mitja. III. Šteger, Aleš
  PGI961.E8A487 2008
  891.8'4808—dc22
                                                    2007052511

1 2 3 4 5 6 7 8 9 UNITED 14 13 12 11 10 09 08

Contents

Introduction

Oh, Slovenia. Yeah, right. Hungarians to the north, Italians to the south. No, that can't be right. Try again: Croatians to the north, Romanians to the south. And Ukraine to the west. Or is it Slovakia? Or Slavonia, rather? Bosnia, perhaps? Yes, that's it. Bosnia to the west. Germany in the heart. And Russia, far, far away. High, uncrossable Alps throwing deep shadows, and the navy in the Slovene sea adding up to three boats, one of them being a rubber dinghy. Oh, Slovenia.

For historians of a biological bent, Slovenes could easily serve as somewhat bizarre proof that even the small not only survive physically; sometimes they are rewarded for their persistence, fanaticism, and incestuous nature: the reward being a state of their own. The Slovene state arose from the wave of post-Communist changes on the map of Europe, where the 1991 ten-day war for independence was an overture to what would be bloody Balkan battles on the territory of the former Yugoslavia. Historically Slovenes had stopped on the crowded crossroads between the Germanic, Romance, and Hungarian worlds to become the westernmost branch of Slavic nations. As a result, the collective memory of the Slovenes is deeply imprinted with centuries of Habsburg rule, later with the Yugoslav monarchy established after World War I, and, finally, with Tito's Socialist experiment following World War II.

During the long centuries without independence, despite the downdraft of history and a permanent cultural inferiority, the Slovene language became recognized as the common sacred emblem of its stubborn and often narrow-hearted speakers. A national awareness was not awakened until the period of Romanticism in the mid-eighteenth century. Since then, it has developed in what could be referred to as a Hegelian spiral. From the beginning of the national awakening process, the nation decisively began to glorify culture, and literature in particular. The lack of national sovereignty was compensated for with the language, and because the language was venerated, a large part of its glory was owed to literature. In Slovenia, the latter is perceived as *belletristic*—that is, as highly praised language in its most aesthetic form. Slovene traditional poetry being highly lyrical and melodic—along with the absence of spectacular epic dimensions—there is nothing strange in the fact that Slovene literature achieved its greatest fruition with a poet and not with a novelist; that is, with the Romantic France Prešeren (1800–1844) and not with the Realist Josip Jurčič (1844–1881).

At the beginning of the nineteenth century, France Prešeren, the eternal legal trainee and bohemian, set himself a truly extravagant task: he wanted to create high literature, comparable to the contemporary models of the time—Goethe, for instance. The extravagance was that he decided to write in a language that seemed to be completely useless for refined expression, and perhaps adequate only for writing practical advice in artisans' handbooks. Actually, Slovene literature does not begin chronologically with Prešeren (the first ever written text in the language known as the precursor of modern Slovene has its roots back in the tenth century); however, the poet's only literary sources of the time were texts of religious, didactical, or derivative nature—that is, texts of no real artistic value. Prešeren passionately invented a language that allowed him to articulate his personal anxiety, which, to a great extent, was rooted in his profound feeling of artistic—that is, intellectual—loneliness in the Slovene society of the time. As a result, one could say that in Prešeren's works there is a combination of worldly desperation, on the one hand, and a faith in his own pioneering mission, on the other. Speaking of the latter, there was a seemingly paradoxical, romantic revolution for Prešeren: his complete loneliness in life was turned into a metaphysical union with the nation. In all his polemics and self-vindications concerning Slovene identity, Prešeren always stood for a positive vision of the nation's future, founded on its being cultivated in the broadest sense. Even nowadays, this kind of attitude is characterized in Slovenia, if less euphorically, as belonging to culture. After his death, Prešeren became the emblem of the nation's self-awakening process. A poet is the prophet of better times. To his followers Prešeren left a double imperative: to write good literature while never forgetting the nation's destiny. The nation's destiny, however, has always floated above the imagination as a kind of corrective or, if you will, a self-censoring device.

Josip Jurčič, the founding father of Slovene prose, was not really indifferent to the nationality of the lady with whom the hero of the first Slovene novel—*Deseti brat (The Tenth Brother)* (1866)—was going to fall in love. If Prešeren's cosmopolitan attitude did not make literature subordinate to ideology, Jurčič introduced another model of national messianism to Slovene literature—linking literary creativity directly with active political engagement. The heritage of this kind of propagandistic and functionalized perception of literature was maintained to the very end of the twentieth century in the works of various Slovene dissident authors. Numerous literary texts that were highly praised for their power of mobilization until recently are, nowadays, only more or less interesting in terms of political history.

Numerous examples will confirm that the public glorification of literature is one thing, while its actual perception is another. At the beginning of the twentieth century, Ivan Cankar (1876–1918), a writer without whom Slovene contemporary literature would not exist, created a series of extraordinary prose and drama works. From Vienna, where he tried his luck, as did so many other Slovene students of that time, he wrote a letter to Zofka Kveder (1878–1926), probably the first important Slovene woman writer: "Home, down there, reformation and revolution in political, social, and public life is needed, and literature should enable this revolution to happen. All is muddy in our homeland."

If Cankar was tormented by adequately distributed *fin-de-siècle* decadence, one could say that the destiny of Srečko Kosovel's avant-garde opus is very telling as well. One of the most significant Slovene poets (1904–1926), Kosovel was torn between his enthusiasm for futurism and a general feeling of horror at the rise of Italian fascism. Despite his early death, he left an astonishingly diversified opus, ranging from impressions of the Karst region to avant-garde experiments. Kosovel's destiny is paradigmatic for the literary perception of the time: after his death, the author became famous for his traditionalist poetry rather than for his more radical constructivist opus, which ended up locked in one of the drawers in the desk of Anton Ocvirk (1907–1980), a well-known professor and the founder of World Literature Studies at Ljubljana University. Kosovel defined the staleness of Slovene literary space with a short four-lined strophe written on the back of the manuscript of his poem "Ljubljana spi" ("Ljubljana's Asleep"):

> Hey, green parrot,
> tell me, how things are in Europe.
> The green parrot replies:
> "man is not symmetrical."

World War II represents a traumatic scar in more recent Slovene history, a scar that is still not completely healed. On the one hand, Slovenes strongly felt the criminality of Nazism and fascism and the bravery of resistance to the ruthless occupation, while on the other they waded into a fratricidal war between the collaborators, who were composed of ancient Yugoslav urban parties and the Slovene branch of the broader people's front led by Tito's Yugoslav Communist Party, which had been virtually anonymous before the war. The violence after the end of the war culminated in serial massacres, in which more than 15,000 militiamen—

that is, soldiers of the former Yugoslav forces—were brutally killed. These *domobranci*, according to the victorious revolutionaries, had by fighting the Communist revolution made a pact with the devil. In the period of postwar Yugoslav Communism, the idea of World War II stuck in the people's subconscious as either a formally glorified myth or a sin completely suppressed on the part of the new leadership.

One fact that bears witness to the trauma of the time is that thirty years had to pass after the bloody postwar massacres and the Communist usurpation of state authority before the Slovene poet and writer Edvard Kocbek (1904–1981) could speak about the bloody postwar events in public. A Catholic Socialist, Kocbek was one of the founders of the liberation movement during the war and a minister in the first Yugoslav government. The pressure on Kocbek weakened only when his destiny was internationalized—that is, when Heinrich Böll became his international supporter and defender.

In opposition to their colleagues in other Communist countries of the time, Slovene writers soon rejected the politically prescribed Socialist Realism. Having overcome the 1948 dispute with Stalin, Yugoslavia engaged in finding a middle course between the East and the West, thus formally allowing more freedom of expression to authors than was permitted in other Eastern bloc nations. Despite certain restrictions, from the middle of the 1960s on, Slovene authors had virtually no lack of information concerning contemporary literary trends in Western Europe. The trend of describing intimate worlds started in the mid-1950s, the time when it represented a certain deviation from a general social collectivization, the most striking example of which were the so-called labor actions, the shock worker campaigns, through which masses of young people all over Yugoslavia engaged in building highways, waterworks, and other infrastructure. Influenced by existentialist philosophy, the modest, intimate literature soon grew into a more ambitious writing: the possibility of expressing more individual visions rooted in metaphor, in the ever-freshly discovered world of parallels that always reflected the climate of the real world—a kind of concrete dome covering an apathetic atmosphere, out of which emerged works on medieval torture, as in Drago Jančar's (b. 1948) novel *Galjot;* or on distant islands of the Adriatic, as in *Filio ni doma (Filio Is Not at Home)* by Berta Bojetu (1946–1997). These authors left a special mark on Slovene postwar prose writing. Beside Jančar and Bojetu, older distinguished authors can be mentioned in this context: Lojze Kovačic (1928–2004), Vitomil Zupan (1914–1987). Florjan Lipuš (1937–), and Boris Pahor (b. 1913).

With rare exceptions, therefore, Slovene literature under Communism never became familiar with the practice of *samizdat,* the clandestine distribution of "subversive" literature that pervaded other Eastern bloc countries. Writers themselves were able to publish their books with state publishing houses; what is more, they could criticize the regime, even if their criticisms were often metaphorical or muffled by the censor or by self-censorship. Literature and the social life related thereto offered room for excess. The authorities' responses were imprisonments and other reprisals on the one hand, and a system of buying relative silence on the other. In the later phase, as the system grew weaker, the writers started proclaiming their doubt-filled ideas more and more loudly. Step by step, metaphors were replaced by direct statements of social and national realities.

The 1970s, and even more intensely the '80s, brought into literature a new literary current. Alongside mainstream modernist literature, which was known for its explicit social criticism, there appeared a new way of writing—writing that was indifferent to the ties of society, paving its own way without social reality as its referential frame. This stimulating escapism tried to find its legitimacy in the maxim "to write literature for literature." This impulse arose against a background of student demonstrations, the hippie movement, pop art, the philosophy of Dušan Pirjevec (a Heideggerian student; 1921–1976), and other factors that promised new modes of creative liberty. A pronounced retreat into the inner worlds of imagination, accompanied by linguistic brilliancies and fantastic, risk-taking plays on words, can be traced to a kind of ultra-modernism whose significant representatives are Uroš Kalčič (b. 1951), Emil Filipčič (b. 1951), and Tone Perčič (b. 1954).

The short prose form has always held an important place in Slovene literature, even if the greatest expectations concerning literature were oriented toward the novel as the great national epic of Tolstoyan origin. The postmodernist softening of discourse in the '80s helped in the affirmation of, and the surge in, short prose. In the period after Tito's death in 1980, the country's society was seized by an ecstatic feeling of liberation and the destruction of the former centers of power. Slovene literature of the time went through the similar process of fragmentation as well. Instead of a Hemingwayesque writer's figure, wandering around to collect the material for his literary creations, Slovene literary iconography now allowed—for the first time—the writer-intellectual, the writer observing the outer world from the distance of his study, doubting whether an authentic event in the modern world were still possible. Or, to put it another way, an academic with a broken pen.

Literature played a powerful symbolic role in Slovenia's gaining independence in 1991. It was the event that revealed a significant heritage from the Communist era, a heritage built upon permanent quarrels between the authors and the system. Independence placed literature on a pedestal; politicians glorified it when making their Sunday speeches. However, in contrast to many expectations, its role in social life was marginalized, even if not entirely. The symbolic collapse of the literary mission certainly brings nothing good in the horrified eyes of older authors, who are used to leading the heroic fight with the regime. The younger generation perceives this change of view and expectations toward literature as a kind of relief. The "wild and passionate" generation of younger authors has taken up the new condition as a creative challenge and not as a reason for apathetic self-pity. If the postwar generation of authors aimed to discover intimacy and rebel against the totalitarian regime, the leading force of Slovene prose in the past fifteen years has been a striving for joy in the cold and ever more globalized modern world. This joy becomes most evident in the vehemence of storytelling, even if the narration itself cannot be described as sly or substantiated by the quantity of information deriving from literary tradition. On the contrary, there is but a seemingly naïve passion for the story, possibly the only one to frame the chaos of our lives. One often has the feeling that these young storytellers were telling extended anecdotes somewhere behind a counter, on a lonely beach, or in the middle of a crowded street. Still, we should not be misled by this sacred simplicity, for it is but a seducing mask, maybe just a kind invitation to listening or reading. That is, younger prose writers do not wish to build hermetically sealed towers to which only the chosen ones would have the key. For them, any retreat to a completely isolated island where they could enjoy their aesthetic games and intellectual gymnastics is impossible. It seems that the reality that surrounds them is simply too dense, neurotic even, and tempting—resembling an unknown landscape full of possible adventures. As a result, they *must be* concerned. Their wish is to break through to the real world, no matter how ordinary or trivial it may be. At the end of the day, therefore, this is why contemporary Slovene literature pulsates so vividly, despite its small market. It is discovering new worlds, nuances of literary language, and, last but not least, the matching literary performances that go together with any kind of literary circus.

If there is no longer one and only metaphysical source of energy centering the world of narration as a whole, there are also no longer any monumental beginnings and denouements of "heroic wanderings." Still, this certainly does not mean that, for example, the emotional processes in the younger prose writing are mere simulations of computer games or culturally conventionalized codes deprived of the power to cut right into the tender flesh. Whatever its various forms or stages of development, love is one of the central themes of the narrative microcosms, ranging from passionate fucking, cursory flirting, fatal attraction, and dull routine to weariness, depression, hatred, and coldness. Love problems and their various disguises will prove that this prose has nothing to do with solipsistic fidgeting on the spot; nor can it be taken as a pile of unambitious fragments having nothing to offer but tinsel under which all is hollow. The problem of loving denotes a perpetual focus and concentration on the other, a perpetual search, a pursuit of the other, sometimes resembling total craziness, at other times indifferent idling; as if a higher form of personal freedom—along with its traps—was hiding only in loving embraces. Here we are talking of freedom as the last-ever heiress of utopia—freedom that, together with love, is probably the most common theme in current prose. Even if the social circumstances have changed, freedom itself has not broadened; and neither have the existential imperatives of the literary hero diminished. The change of climate conditions only seems to have brought different strategies for encircling freedom, different obstacles to overcome. Drinking, drugs, crazy driving, all-night conversations, wandering about, violence—all of that, and more and more of such actions—may be nothing else but different ways that promise some patch or other of liberated land. This may appear somewhere unexpectedly in between or on the border of moments.

The stories gathered in this book were written between 1990 and 2005. Although the poetics of the writers represented here are quite different, they are united by their constant concern with the status of reality—on one hand, completely eroded by doubts, and on the other naïvely recalled as authenticity, even if only behind a counter, in an anonymous street, or in an apartment block. The turn toward verity, which bites its own tail, the transition from the metaphorical to the metonymical, has numerous forms. In most cases, these are instance of the unsustainable and insidious duality, a grammatical particularity of the Slovene language that even the majority of native speakers have difficulty mastering, let alone those for whom it is less well known. Still, if you, dear distant reader, alone or in pairs, manage to find us there, in the nowhere, to the west of Bosnia, to the left of Italy, we hope you will enjoy the reading.

MITJA ČANDER and ALEŠ ŠTEGER

A Note on the Translations

The translations as they appear in this collection came to us from a variety of hands—most of them directly from native Slovene speakers, and only three from a native English speaker. As a result, while many of the original translations of these stories were good—and a few were very, very good—rarely did the Slovene-speaking translator produce a text that read like the English of a native English speaker (be this the English of Britain, where I grew up, or the English of North America, where I have lived for nearly forty years).

I admit that, when faced with a source translation that did not read as if it came from a native English speaker, in the editing process I may have tended to be too exact in my judgments in order to compensate. Therefore, I may have made corrections where the versions I was dealing with were in spirit close to their originals, and hence where corrections were perhaps not really essential. Indeed, more than a few of the translations—although not "reading quite right," and sounding in one way or another foreign to the English ear—did indeed capture much of the artistic intent of the original authors. It was always my intent to retain the essence of the original story, while at the same time providing a final version that sounds as naturally "English" as possible. This often called for decisions to favor one over the other, and in such instances I favored the English of the target audience.

TOM PRIESTLY

angels
beneath
the surface

The Fall of the House of Pirnat

MAJA NOVAK

*I*t all began innocently enough. What happened was nothing worse than this: Robbie Pirnat leaned a little too far over the railing of the sixth-floor balcony and fell. And a stranger happened to be passing by who did not hesitate—not that he had time to think, and who knows what he might have decided had he had the time—who did not hesitate to place himself where the child was about to land, and who opened his arms wide. A millionth of a second later, the two of them were rolling around on the ground. The stranger had cracked ribs; Robbie was screaming like a guy selling strawberries in the street.

And then all at once, on the expanse of asphalt at the foot of the six high-rises, there appeared, out of thin air, an ant colony of people, as if God had improvised them for this very moment; and then—granted, a little late, but with their whole heart in it—Robbie's parents arrived, shouting. In their excitement, they doubtless would have caused more harm than good had they been able to push their way through the throng to Robbie and his savior. With that customary yelp that the brain registers as mute bluish thunderbolts behind the eyes, two ambulances roared up. Into the first went Robbie, who was perfectly fine, except frightened to death; and the stranger, hugging himself to hold his ribs in place, followed after. They took the stranger gently by the shoulders and showed him that the second ambulance was the one meant for him, but no, he insisted, no, he wanted to ride with the boy, he had saved his life and so he was responsible for him, or at least he had to carry out his duties to the very end, he had to, no two ways about it, go to the hospital with the boy and sit in the emergency room waiting for news of the boy's condition; and then when that was taken care of—he said—he could return by bus, because he didn't have the money for a taxi, and let the second ambulance take him away so they could have a look at his ribs, too. They had a hard time convincing him that that was not the way things worked.

The TV crew was at the hospital ahead of the ambulance. *Cinema verite* style, they got the mother's face, puffy from the crying and ten years of comfort food; and they got a nice pan of the father's hairy arm laid patronizingly across the mother's shoulder, that lady, from behind a mountain of soggy paper hankies, in a strangulated voice told the camera that she was so grateful, but, really, so grateful to the stranger, she couldn't even say how grateful, she would do anything, but anything, for him, and she meant anything, to repay him; forever they would keep him in their thoughts and in their hearts, forever they would remember him in their prayers, his picture they would put on the piano in the living room and surround it with flowers, and on wintry days, with the apartment nice and warm, they would show this picture to their grandchildren (Robbie's potential children) and would tell them solemnly, resonantly, as if reminding them of an ancient family oath, "If it wasn't for this man, you wouldn't be here either."

The director was happy. At the head of a parade of lighting guys, cameramen, and the guy carting the camera, he headed for the rescuer, because now he wanted more. The rescuer had just been wrapped in a mile of bandages, and his name was Bootso and he was Bosnian. Bootso, the Bosnian.

They asked him what he thought about everything, how he liked his noble role and all.

"A *shta bih*, what else?" said Bootso, shrugging his shoulders. This far into his speech he spoke his language, but, hey, everyone understood.

"Anyone would have done the same," he added when they kept at him. This he said in Slovenian. He had learned, hadn't he, after his years up here?

They asked him how he felt.

"How? Good," he said, he said bilingually, after giving it some thought. He seemed surprised, amazed that people thought there was some way to feel other than good.

Did he have any special desires?

"No, I don't," he said in his language, but everyone understood. He was surprised. And then after a pause longer than the last, as if uncertain of the ethical and logical appropriateness of the sentence he was about to utter, he added hesitantly, "Maybe, I guess, what I want is for the youngster to get better as fast as he can."

Given the communicational inhibitions of the performer, this part of the reportage was quite a bit shorter than the first.

But it was plenty lots, together with the moving image of mother-in-tears, for Mrs. Pirnat to be bathed in tears again two days later in front of the TV. In tears for all the woe she had suffered, and in her frayed voice—the one that her consort and the elder son and the daughter and Robbie had long ago learned to obey more quickly than the sharpest command—in her frayed voice, she suggested that, to show their gratitude, they should invite this saintly man to supper.

If she had had any idea what she was getting into, she would no doubt have jumped off the balcony herself.

For the rest of the week, they ate *canard à l'orange,* because that was what was planned for the formal dinner with guest, and Mrs. Pirnat had never done duck before and she didn't want it to turn out badly the night Bootso, the honored guest, would be there, so she needed to practice a little. They bought candles, they consulted about the wine, and then, on the night of nights, they sat down around the table and waited. They waited the fifteen minutes you give a professor late for his lecture; and then another quarter hour, and then a third. The duck, which in this latest test had turned out really fine, was covered now with a sticky crust of fat; and, then, an hour plus another half-hour later, somebody laid the weight of his whole body on the doorknob to the apartment, which action had no effect whatever, because the door was locked. This same someone then bypassed the door bell, nor did he knock; he slammed his shoulder into the door because he couldn't for the life of him imagine that the door of the apartment to which you are invited to supper could possibly be locked. So the elder Pirnat son graciously lifted himself from the table and went to unlock the door; the hostess pattered after him, first secretly adjusting the position of the vase, expecting, it goes without saying, the bouquet the guest would bring. And in marched Bootso, unaware that he was late, as a matter of fact he didn't know such a concept of time existed; in he came and pushed into the bosom of the hostess—actually she intercepted it just ahead of her bosom—a bottle of slivovitz, wrapped in newspaper. The vase sighed in disappointment and died.

"We were afraid you weren't coming," said Papa Pirnat, throwing out the hook that was supposed to land excuses.

"Not come? But, people, we said we were having supper, right?" He spoke half in his language, half in Slovenian, believing himself to be speaking Slovenian. The Slovenians, proud of their linguistic abilities, believed he was speaking his language.

At any rate, fine, the guest is always right, especially if he's saved your son's life. You have to be patient with him, you have to understand him. He's underprivileged, it's not his fault he doesn't know manners, at any rate, we Pirnats are neither racists nor fuddy-duddies; acting as a unit, they steered him over to the table. He sat down and lit a cigarette using the candle.

"Ahem. You know, we're all nonsmokers at our house," Mama Pirnat opened the conversation affably. (*Dictionary of the Slovenian Literary Language, DSLL*, Volume III, p. 720: *pogovor (conversation)*: 1. Something you have to do, especially at formal suppers.)

Replying with like affability, except that his sentiments were real, Bootso in amazement said, "No? Oh no, don't tell me you're sick?"

They were silent, feeling that the conversation was slipping out of their hands.

But, hey, Bootso figured it out for himself.

"Oh, I get it, you don't have an ashtray. Not to worry, lady. A plate'll do fine."

Ahem.

(Three weeks later, in the elevator, the woman next door gave Mrs. Pirnat the tongue lashing of her life. What was she doing inviting people who in this very same elevator smoke like chimneys, like Turks, and, what's more, who do not stop smoking when, with eyebrows raised, you let them know that such interference with the rights and liberties of fellow passengers is the sort of thing the ombudsman should look into. But this was only three weeks later.)

Then the duck marched onstage, a little stiff, it should be added, from rigor mortis. Bootso takes a leg in his hands and chews and chews and chews. The others eat, too, though they've had it up to here with *canard à l'orange.*

"Don't belch," quoth Papa Pirnat to Robbie.

"So why can he?" asks Robbie, rocking on his chair, watching Bootso with great interest.

Bootso is chewing; he chews with concentration, undisturbed by what goes on around him.

Robbie smiles at Bootso, Bootso smiles at Robbie. They like each other, they do. The Pirnats' daughter, seventeen, flares her nostrils theatrically.

The rest of the family suffers bravely; he saved their son, they are grateful, what are these trivia to them? They want to converse with him (*DSLL*, III, 720: *pogovarjati se (to converse):* letting someone know through conversation that he is not unwanted). What's the use? Bootso hasn't read the *DSLL*, he does not know how to converse, he opens his mouth only when he really sincerely has something to say, for instance, "Good duck, lady, except too bad you put it in the orange juice. Next time try it with just the fat, you'll see, it'll be better."

The Pirnats feel trapped: they've had it with their guest, but what to do? He saved their son, they don't dare pass judgment, they wouldn't dare hate him, so they observe him and look painstakingly for something about him to like. Robbie has already found this something, but, hey, Robbie is six, his discoveries and his value judgments he still expresses so incoherently he's hardly in a position to advise. There are the Pirnats, stealing glances, passing messages with their eyes, insisting, swearing, promising, guaranteeing, convincing one another and themselves, that Bootso is one great guy (he saved their son); all that is needed is to get to know him better, and they will find, beneath the rough exterior, pure gold. So, finally, after they have managed to pour some of the slivovitz into themselves, because Bootso insists and will not take no for an answer (he did bring it with the best of intentions, didn't he?), and after they have all managed to quell their belching, somebody says (and there will later be much quarreling about just who it was that pulled the stupid stunt), "Please, will you come again next week?"

Now Bootso has a problem; they're nice, the family, the supper was fine, the kid he saved is cute, he's got nothing against the Pirnats, but, if the truth be told, he would a week from today prefer to be in his rooming house, in front of the TV, because the Italians are playing the Dutch, and there he would be sitting quietly, with a bottle of warm beer in his hand, naked to the waist, unwashed, surrounded by his buddies, maybe, from the construction site, safely wrapped in the communal silence and the impregnable curtain of smoke, but, hey, duty is duty. He saved their child, he became a part of their lives and they a part of his, and a link like that only death can break, what has to be has to be, so the invitation causes him some problems, but it's not like it's causing him pain deep down in his soul, and so, as decisively as he caught their boy, he accepts the invitation for a week from tonight.

MAJA NOVAK

Tomi, the elder son, sixteen years old and a cynic, says to Robbie after the door has shut, has been locked, has been bolted behind Bootso, "The next time you fall off the balcony, make sure there's nobody underneath."

For this he receives a formative shot in the mouth.

Mama Pirnat buries her face behind her polished fingernails and weeps, as she has not wept since the day she lost her virginity, and the seventeen-year-old laughs sneakily, as she has not laughed since the day she lost hers.

Paterfamilias calls a war council.

You have to be gentle with Bootso, he says to the older heirs; you have to understand him, you have to empathize with his inner self, his world, his thoughts, his difficulties; they must—you understand, you must, you, Tomi, you, following the liberal arts path in high school, you will one day have to know that this is what is known as the categorical imperative—they have to connect with him, break through the communicational blockade, bridge the cultural differences, the hundreds of years of cultural differences, they have to start talking with him, that is to say, uttering utterances that really mean something; that's it, that's what needs doing, they have to live in his life, and then it will become clear to all of them what a really wonderful person Bootso is.

Sure, empathize, enter his world, but how?

What they are really doing is feverishly mining for some noble characteristic, any noble characteristic, that might help them be grateful to him, yes, but, they ask and ask themselves in terror, how can you understand what noble instinct it is that drives you to come late to supper, to terrorize nonsmokers, to criticize the hostess's cooking, though just moments before you were smacking your lips and belching and licking your fingers; what noble instinct makes you guzzle that slivovitz, that disgusting, that … after which all you can do is belch, dammit, though that's not acceptable, of course … ? That Bootso might beyond all this do some other things, with which they could perhaps empathize, occurs, of course, to none of them in their blessed simplicity. And so, like a cat chasing its tail, they fruitlessly twirl around for a week trying to solve the enigma named Bootso.

With a similar lack of success, they rummage about looking for themes that they might broach with this good, if somewhat difficult, person who saved their son.

"You're the scholar, Tomi, be constructive," snaps Father.

"What about religion?" Tomi suggests with the voice and the face of a professional poker player. "How's about if we try to get inside his faith? He's a Muslim, right?"

"Buy the Koran and start studying," the Father orders, for the *n*th time falling for one of his son's practical jokes.

Tomi buys a Koran, folio edition, and spends a week looking at porn he hides inside. And gets away with it; at the supper that the Pirnats have been anticipating with a lump in their throats as if awaiting a second chance at an exam they've flunked, there isn't time for one single word about Islam. Because Bootso shows up with a cheap plastic car, a tiny tiny car, but which rides around like a real one and which is to Robbie, the recipient, an endless source of joy; he shows up with that and a small, banged-up transistor, which he places by his plate and then amid loud slurping (this time it's *pasul*, bean stew, one of *his* dishes and cheaper than French stuff) he listens at maximum volume to the Italians playing the Dutch, dead to the rest of the world.

"I hope this doesn't bother you," he asks them affably in his native tongue, at halftime.

They understand, and understandingly say that it doesn't.

Nor do they surrender. Fine, so they'll try to enter his world (it doesn't occur to them a suitable subject might be soccer) next week. At supper.

It is after that supper that the protest in the elevator is registered. Then, during the fourth, Tomi, who has secretly been smoking since the seventh grade, pulls out a pack, at just the moment when Bootso lights his fifteenth cigarette; the guest understandingly offers him his cigarette, for the boy to light up at its smoldering tip. When Bootso has taken his farewell, Mother Pirnat takes a fit and accuses the savior of her younger lambkin of being responsible for the moral degeneration of her older. The ram hasn't the slightest intention of explaining how things really stand with him and smoking. "Empathizing," is all he says, shrugging his shoulders.

After the fifth supper, the neurotic seventeen-year-old Pirnat filly tattles out loud that Bootso has been trying to get her into bed. Just before the mother has a heart attack, Father Pirnat intervenes in the all-around howling and in what he says there is a surprisingly large portion of good sense: maybe Bootso meant less than he said, perhaps the girl imagined more than she heard, as for that it is not entirely impossible that the brat thought the whole thing up. *In dubio pro reo*, adds Pirnat, who is a lawyer; what have we got left except to comfort ourselves with doubt since we've invited him to supper number six, anyways.

"I can't take it anymore," says Mrs. Pirnat in her frayed voice, the one against which there is no appeal, she says this the night before the last supper, "I can't take it anymore, and that's that, I know we invited him, I know it's only right, he did rescue the child, it's not his fault that he is the way he is, poor man, but my nerves are shot, you all know I'm not a chauvinist, I have nothing against feeding and watering him once a week, we have to be grateful, I would do anything for him, why I would bathe him, and he does need it, but this is it, I've had it, I cannot survive one more supper, *basta.*" And she weeps.

"There, there, Mother," says Mr. Pirnat.

"These suppers with Bootso must stop," adds Tomi in a manly voice. "They must stop tonight."

"Oh yeah, so what are you going to say to him?" suddenly bursts out the seventeen-year-old, the very one from whom for a while now nobody has expected anything, the one who, if the truth be known, is the family champion in entering Bootso's world, "What're you going to say to him, 'Molim lepo (she breaks into the language of Bootso's world), please, next Sunday don't show up.' You know what he's going to say? (She breaks into sort of his language again.) He'll say, 'But, people, why not?'" She finishes in Slovenian. "That's exactly what he's going to say and he'll look stunned on top of it all."

"You're probably right," murmurs the father, "and the truth we can't tell him, because we would hurt his feelings...."

"... If he's got any ..."

"You keep quiet, Tomi; as I said, if he has feelings, we mustn't hurt those...."

"... We can't just say nothing either," the daughter continues passionately," because if we only say good-bye without singing that regular chorus of ours, 'Come again next week,' he will, despite the fact that we haven't specifically invited him, I mean, despite the fact that we have specifically not invited him, despite that, he'll show up in a week's time on his own, the way he always does, right on time...."

"Right on time?"

"Well, you know what I mean."

"Valium," rasps the mother, pointing with her manicured nails at the drawer of the night table, "Valium ..."

"What if we pushed him off the balcony? Or killed him with food poisoning? I bet Mom could pull that off.... The dead don't have feelings we can hurt." From Tomi.

For five seconds they quite seriously weigh this option.

"Nah, we can't," Tomi finally decides. "He is still human, after all."

"And we are human, too, and that is why we do not kill other humans," agrees the categorical imperative expert, Papa Pirnat.

There followed about ten pages worth of silence.

"May I suggest a liberal arts-path solution," the enlightened Tomi finally spoke up. "Let's lie. It's simple; we smile, we look him in the eye, and we wail a little: Dearest Bootso, our hearts are broken, but next week we cannot meet, for we will not be in town, we're going to the cottage, we have to, you know, quite unexpectedly a great misfortune has befallen us, the roof of the garage has caved in. And it did, right, four years ago?"

"Are you going to bring up the damn roof again? Did I or did I not buy the lumber to fix it?" Father Pirnat.

"Yes, you did. It's been lying there four years now." Mother Pirnat. The change of theme does her nerves a ton of good.

The seventeen-year-old, off in her own world, is playing with the Valium box, wondering whether she dares light up a cigarette in front of her mother. "So what are you going to say if you run into him on the street and you're supposed to be at the cottage?" she says.

"Who says I'm going to run into him?"

Another volcanic eruption: "Because he's everywhere, don't you understand, the city is full of him, they're everywhere these guys, that's why he was under the balcony when Robbie fell." She lights her cigarette, nobody notices.

"Fine," says Tomi, "so we'll really go to the cottage."

"What, I'm supposed to throw away my precious vacation so that I can go fix the damn roof?"

"Well, it is about time. . . ." Mama Pirnat, once more.

"Cool down, old man; you don't have to fix anything; you'll be at the cottage, in your bathing suit and in your socks, lying on the rubber raft in front of the portable TV, Mom'll be warming up the cans on the little heater, my cow of a sister will be taking the sun, and me and Robbie we'll go looking for mushrooms and then fish, we'll relax, all of us, and no Bootso anywhere, do you understand, no Bootso. Christ, say something, yes or no?"

Yes or no? Yes! And how!

The flowers are singing, the birds are blooming, the Pirnats are at the cottage, the sun's rays pierce through whispering treetops, the lumber is busy drying on the lee side of the white, white cottage, *requiescat in pacem.* Mother lifts her eyes from her embroidery and a shriek of horror escapes from her throat. Bootso is coming up the gravel driveway. A knapsack on his back, a toolbox in one hand, wearing his blue workday overalls he is, a hole in one of the knees.

"*Zdravo, ljudi.*" In all his glory he speaks to them in his native tongue. "Hello, people, here I am, I've come to help you with the roof."

His face is aglow; he has not been this happy in a long, long time, this is the real thing, here he can be useful, he's really had his fill of the suppers, he'd missed England against the Spaniards, he'd missed, wait for it, *Cibona* against *Makabi,* his buddies from the construction site are making fun of him, lovely, lovely, what a gentleman he's become, we're not good enough for him any more, they don't understand, he saved their son and now the Slovenians are his family, and a family is a family in good times and bad, you have to accept it the way Allah gave it to you, you can't complain about it, but a man has to do something to take care of his family, too, make something nice for them, something real, that bit with the little one that was nothing, anybody would have done it, and then they were so nice to him, he's been thinking and thinking what he might do for them and here it is, their roof caved in, and what, they're intellectuals, right, they're Slovenians, what do they know about things like that, people like that, and he's a trained carpenter, if they don't need him now, then when?

And he says to them in his native tongue, "*Aymo ljudi,* let's go, people, let's get to work." In Slovenian he then says to Mr. Pirnat, "First-class wood, you've got there. It's as if it's been drying for four years."

He scurries like a squirrel up to the roof of the garage, he's whistling, he makes himself a pulley and brings the wood up, he works on the rafters, he's nailing down the lumber, the hammer sings, Bootso sings. "Brew me up some coffee, *dusho* (soul of mine)." (What a language, eh?) One warm beer after another disappears down his gullet. "Okay, boss, jump in your car and bring us another twenty-four." Now he's covering the pine with the Canadian asphalt shingles. "All right, young lady, wake up, you've got the legs, go get me some more." He sweats like a horse, he does everything himself, he's in a hurry, it wasn't easy getting a week off from the construction site. The Pirnats do what they can, hey, everybody's got to pitch in, calluses pop open, there's sawdust in their hair, boy have they got a pain in their backs. Then the week of construction is over, the precious vacation has ended. The roof now—that roof is the sort of roof no garage has ever seen the likes of. They return to the city, they give Bootso a ride, of course, the man hasn't got the money to be spending it needlessly on buses. They drop him off at the rooming house (invite him to supper in a week's time), they just have the energy to drive the car around the corner and Father Pirnat collapses on the steering wheel, and Mother Pirnat lowers her head to the dashboard.

"You can go ahead and tell me I am an ungrateful sow," she howls angrily, "but there will be no sign of me here a week from today."

"Where can we hide?" the children ask practically.

"Turn around, it's back to the cottage," says Tomi decisively.

"Are you crazy?" his sister screams. "He'll find us there just like that."

They decide on a motel on the coast, in Ankaran.

And when a week later they throw open the shutters and are rubbing their sleepy eyes, looking in the direction of every Slovenian citizen's birthright, 15 inches of beach sand and muddy sea, their eyes on the misty sun, whom do they see smiling at them from behind a bottle of warm beer, sitting under the awning of the café on the other side of the parking lot?

"Hello, people, here I am, I've come to invite you to supper tonight, my treat." In his language, which they understand.

He's picked out the place and everything, a really nice little grill on the beach, they serve *chevapchichi* and *dzhulbastiya* and kidney bean stew, all you can eat.

Before dawn next morning, the Pirnats flee to Postoyna, of the world famous caves and stuff.

And that's about it.

For whom should they espy, peeking out, elf-like from behind transparent stalactites and jewel-like stalagmites, from behind the veil of ringing water drops in the world famous cave? And then whose shadow is it falls over the picture of paradise they see while floating on Lake Bled? Who is that strolling in the old town in Maribor when the Pirnats are strolling there too? Who is that sliding down the water slide at the spa in Chateshke Hot Springs? Whose footsteps echo under the vaults and down the corridor in the priory at Stichna where the Pirnats are seeking peace and spiritual solace? Who *is* that person hiding under the cloak of the Blessed Virgin in the pilgrims' church at Ptuyska Mountain? Who is the young man laughing in the vineyard in Dolensko? Who comes riding up on a Lippizaner to meet their carriage, who comes galloping, rather, for didn't he learn to ride, bareback, before he got his first pair of pants? Who is drinking a cup of coffee guess where, and who is the only vertical standing out from the horizontal of the blue poppy fields at Beltintsy? But that's enough of a list, tourist brochures we have aplenty, thank you, on this sunny side of the Alps, too many, and some more depressing than this text.

The Pirnats were last seen in Szombathely, Hungary, at the exact moment when Bootso was spotted crossing the Slovenian-Hungarian border at Dolga Vas. Mother Pirnat is talking divorce and the seventeen-year-old is planning her getaway with a croupier she met in one of Slovenia's famous casinos at some point in the family's flight.

Fact is, good sex can heal the worst spiritual traumas.

And now a final sentence—

—Listen I know it's going to sound pathetic and pretentious, but I can't help it, we are who we are, I've got to write it down, I came up with it by myself, about philosophy I know about as much as Papa Pirnat, so it's not like I copied it from Lacan or Hobbes or Wittgenstein (or, rather,

tell me, what philosopher is currently the latest thing in Slovenia?), whatever, here it is—

—We can never enter fully into another's being; we can't read anyone's thoughts; we can never understand somebody else, at best we can
learn them by heart, and if sometimes it seems to us that we predicted
correctly what somebody was going to do it's merely a phenomenon of
statistical probability; nobody is anything other than an island, the situation is hopeless, and one fine morning for no reason at all we're going
to smother one another with the whitest duvet while we're asleep.

Translated by TOM LOZAR

History Is Written by the Winner

DUŠAN ČATER

The armchair did not provide much cover. She had hit him twice already, one time really close to his left eye. That had really scared him. He had run out of rubber bands, too, while she, inexplicably, still seemed to have a fistful. His predicament was indeed unenviable.

"Sara, listen!" he said. "Let's call it quits!"

He heard only her laughter. There was something terrifying in it, or so it seemed to him.

"Sara, listen …"

Nothing. Just rubber bands whizzing past him. One of them landed quite close, and when he reached for it, another one struck his hand. It hurt a great deal, and in his mind he used some very bad language. He nevertheless managed to pick it up and loaded his gun by hooking the rubber band at one end of the weapon, then stretching it and fixing it taut with the clothespin attached at the other end. Thus equipped he waited for the right moment, feeling like a soldier carefully saving his last bullet. Which is probably what it was.

Sara, his wife, continued to shoot at him, but that did not bother him much now. He was well hidden, and all the rubber bands whizzed either over him or past him. He was only worried in case the whole thing lasted too long, because he badly needed to empty his bladder. The thought of surrendering crossed his mind, but that would entail dire consequences. Last time she had tied him up really tightly and extracted all possible confessions from him by force.

He opted for a ruse.

"Sara," he tried, "you've hurt me. I can hardly feel my hand. You're better than me. I give up!"

Sara chuckled. This time a fraction less terrifyingly, and he also heard her get up. He did not want to lift his head, because he knew she was holding her weapon in front of her, loaded and ready to fire. When she came up to him, he first stared at her legs and feet, until he finally lifted his eyes. She was smiling a bit like a movie star, with the corners of her lips curled up.

"What's new?" she asked.

"Actually," he said, and with a sudden movement he swung at her. With his left hand he swiped at her weapon, and the rubber band zipped into the television set. At the same moment he drew his own gun from behind his back, and just like that, from below, hit her right in the eye. Sara cried out and dropped her weapon onto the carpet. He kicked it across the room and lunged at her. When he'd wrestled her under him, he sat on her. He extricated a rubber band from her tightly clenched fist and cocked his gun. He aimed it straight at her eye and said, "What news have you got for me, sweetheart?"

"You're a cunt, Mister Arnelly," she said, and he knew she was embarrassed about the defeat.

When they were drinking coffee a little while later, and blowing thick cigarette smoke toward the ceiling, Mister Arnelly held his hand on her knee, while she held her eye.

"What else do you want?" she asked.

"Tell me what she told you yesterday!"

Sara rolled her good eye.

"But I've told you already she doesn't want to speak to you," she said.

Mister Arnelly put out his cigarette in the ashtray.

"But she speaks to you!" he said.

"Not about you, though," she said.

"It doesn't matter anyway. I never cared much for there being three of us," he said.

"Don't say that!"

Mister Arnelly rose to refill his coffee cup. When he was in the kitchen he heard the doorbell. He knew she had come to visit. Lately she'd been coming here virtually every day. Ostensibly she was a bit worried about her mother and all that. With his coffee cup in his hand he went to stand in the doorway. Sara and their daughter were seated on the sofa. A little to the side stood a burly young man.

"You haven't lost again, have you?" the daughter asked.

Sara nodded.

"What lie did he use to beat you this time?"

"He said he was hurt!"

"Again?! Oh, Mom …"

"He was very convincing," said Sara.

The daughter looked at him, still standing in the doorway, still holding his cup.

"You old son of a bitch!" she said.

Then she turned to her big boyfriend and said, "You'd never pull a thing like that off. You're not depraved enough!"

The beefy young man shifted his weight from one foot to the other and cracked his knuckles.

She turned back to Sara and asked, "Did you tell him anything, Mom?"

Sara shook her head and gave her a secret wink.

Mister Arnelly went to the sofa, sat down and lit another cigarette. He listened to them as they talked about things he knew nothing about, but he did not let that bother him. He knew, somehow he simply knew, that Sara, his wife, would eventually tell him everything. After all, he was the winner.

Translated by TAMARA M. SOBAN

The Love Seat

DUŠAN ČATER

Mister Arnelly paused outside the door, extracted his key from his pocket, and unlocked the door. When he opened it, he heard music coming from the living room. He took off his shoes, left them outside the closet, and went into the living room. Sara, his wife, was dancing barefoot on the love seat.

He was barefoot too.

He looked at her and went past her into the kitchen. He opened the fridge and took out a bottle of juice. He took a glass from the sink and rinsed it. He poured himself one.

Sara came in after him.

"So?" she asked.

"Turn down the radio," he said.

She went and turned down the volume.

"So?" she asked again when she came back.

"It's your turn to say it," he told her.

"No, I think it's your turn today!"

"No, it isn't!"

"I said it yesterday!"

"Don't lie. I distinctly remember: As I was putting my shoes in the closet, scared because they were dirty, right then I said that I loved you!"

"That's right, I remember now!"

"So?"

"I love you, Arnelly, you fat-butt!" Sara said.

He kissed her on the cheek.

She ran into the living room, turned the volume all the way up and leapt onto the love seat. He heard the springs groan.

He sat down at the table and lit a cigarette. He washed down the first drag with juice.

"Did you eat yet?" he called to her.

"What?"

"Did you eat?"

"No, I'm not going to eat today," she said.

Mister Arnelly put out his half-smoked cigarette and went to stand in the doorway. He watched her bouncing about on the love seat. Their eyes met and he accepted the invitation. He jumped up to join her and together they bounced up and down on the love seat. Barefoot and in time with the music.

First they held hands, then they let go. Next she made a turn, then he did. Then she again and he again. She and he. Sara and Mister Arnelly, the fat-butt. She laughed, he laughed. They danced.

"Wait," he said and strained his ears.

"What is it?"

"I think it's the phone," he said.

He hopped off the love seat and turned down the radio. There was ringing coming from the hall.

"Oh, my God," Sara said.

He nodded to her compassionately and went to the telephone. He lifted the receiver.

"Yes?" he said.

Silence.

Mister Arnelly nodded his head and said, every so often, "Yes, of course, when ... yes ... tomorrow then ... uh-huh ... okay ... bye!"

Sara was looking at him, frightened. He nodded to her. He was truly sorry.

Sara hid her face in her hands and sobbed. He caressed her short cropped hair and went past her into the kitchen. He sat down at the table and lit a cigarette. He thought about how there were no words with which he could comfort her. He sat and smoked. He stared into space and blew smoke toward the ceiling.

Sara sat down next to him. Her eyes were red.

"Tomorrow then, is it?" she said.

"Yeah, tomorrow," he said.

"Arnelly, you fat-butt! I love you!" she said and wanted to smile, but just moaned a little, her throat constricted.

The following day, right after Mister Arnelly put his dirty shoes away in the closet and called out "I love you!" in the direction of the living room, some workmen in white overalls took the love seat, loaded it onto a truck and hauled it away.

Sara turned down the radio. For good!

Translated by TAMARA M. SOBAN

Independence Day

ANDREJ BLATNIK

his is the story Papa will tell me. Papa, who'll know for a long time to come how it was in the old days without you and me, at a time when you couldn't accept a candy from a stranger in the street because it was poisoned for sure, in those days when it was only strangers in the street who had candies, and you couldn't accept them if you wanted to stay alive, this is a story from the end of that time and you have to hear it too, and listen to it so that you can pass it on to your children when the time comes. That's why I'm confiding it to you, and the two of us will speak guardedly, in an undertone, choosing our words with care, as befits those days of old, and we'll glance over our shoulders in case there's somebody there eavesdropping on what is none of their business.

He was there, Papa will tell me, he was right there in the first row, right up in the front, and the cork that popped uncontrollably from one of the numerous bottles of champagne hit none other than him as he pushed his way toward the platform, stretching his hand holding a hard-won glass up to the stage, and the cork left a blackish bruise above his eye. Since accidents never come alone, as the proverb says, in surprise he let go of his frantic hold on the glass, which shattered on the ground, and Papa, stumbling, fell on his stretched-out hand and then, as soon as the people drew back enough for him to pick himself up, he saw the criss-cross of blood on his palm.

There were a few screams, nobody had expected blood, not on a day they had been anticipating year after year, generation after generation, lifetime after lifetime, they all knew it was possible, though nobody had expected it to actually happen, but it happened, things like that do happen, it's okay though, no harm done, everybody around him said, so in the end Papa said it too, what else could he do, it's okay, he said, and people laughed, patting his shoulders, it's okay, it's okay, they called out all around, while his palm dripped blood and hurt, it's okay, he said through clenched teeth, he kept repeating it, and then he accepted the proffered glass of brandy and downed it in one gulp, as fast as possible, and it really began to seem that it had to be okay since everybody said so, himself included, that there could be no harm, although the palm of his hand smarted oddly.

With the second glass it became crystal clear to him that everything was indeed okay, really and truly, if there had been something that was not okay, that was before, but it was okay now and would always be okay, so he didn't resist much when that girl started kissing him, it was quite acceptable, there was plenty of kissing going on all around, it was a special time like never before and possibly never again, and it's hard to hold back if everyone else is kissing, in particular with a girl who doesn't even try to hold you back, but quite to the contrary puts her hand on your bruise, puts it there so often that the pain disappears and is replaced by another feeling, pleasant and unknown. And that's why Papa didn't resist when this girl whispered to him that it was really too crowded here and that even here, in the old part of town—oh, not just a town anymore, as of tonight the capital—there were plenty of hidden corners that have been there forever, waiting forever for couples like them. And that's why Papa followed her, that's why he let her take him by the hand and lead him into one of those dark hallways whose reason for being might be that in them people can discharge or inject fluids, into one of those hallways whose murky darkness screens out unwanted stares, and you know what happened in that hallway, things like that happen to everyone, or nearly everyone, in particular on days like that which had never occurred before and will never occur again.

ANDREJ BLATNIK

He doesn't remember much, Papa will tell me, he doesn't recall exactly what happened to him in that hallway, it was over so fast, faster than he thought or wished, but it felt nice, pleasant, it felt the way it should on a very special day, the kind of day one experiences for the first time, if they do at all, that is, because it seems, Papa will mention, that there are also people to whom these things never happen, but such people, Papa will add, don't really know what they've missed, and so possibly they don't feel so bad about it as they would if they did.

The one thing he does recall, though, Papa will also tell me, is that when they picked up their things and went back outside, under the independent sky, a woman spoke to them, a woman dragging behind her some cardboard boxes tied together with a piece of string. Excuse me, do you two perhaps live in a box, she asked, and Papa recalls shaking his head, he recalls looking in his woman's eyes and unexpectedly seeing them fill with horror. Then give me some change, the cardboard-box woman said, seizing the chance, and Papa recalls reaching into his pocket without hesitation, expecting to find something there—but there was nothing, he had left everything at the stands where champagne was served, nothing was free, not even on a day like this, is anything ever free if nothing is free on a day like this, he recalls reaching into his pocket and not finding anything there, and his woman took him by the hand, no, no, she said, although he himself had also felt no, that wouldn't do, even though he might have wished that it would. And he recalls, Papa will finally tell me, how they went on together, he and this woman from the hallway, his woman for the night, with whom he was to become a couple, but not right away, not that night, oh, no, quite some time would go by, first they would circle around each other, pondering whether they should or shouldn't, but then they found out about me and finally owed up that they were a couple, Papa will finish, and how they walked on and how the cardboard-box woman followed them with her eyes, looking at them for a long time, before she began arranging her cardboard boxes in the hallway, that hallway they had just vacated.

ANGELS BENEATH THE SURFACE

This is the story Papa will tell me when I ask how I came into this world, and he'll tell it to me softly, as though embarrassed about things being the way they were, about his palm bleeding and about not finding anything when he reached in his pocket. And I won't understand why he's embarrassed, just as you don't understand why I'm embarrassed when I tell you this story, and just as your children won't understand you when the time comes for them to know about it.

But that is still far in the future, let's leave that for you, you can deal with that when the time comes. Another story is about to happen, I can't hold back any longer, my day is coming. I'm about to come into the world, I'll delight in the gust of air that will penetrate my body, it will be all different from inside here, it will be all unknown and large, different, that's good, it can't be anything but good, and I'll scream for joy. The woman I'll later, much later, learn to call Mom will be there, gasping somewhere in the background, What is this? I'll ask myself, What's going on? Why doesn't that voice shut up? And Papa will lean close to me, he'll touch me, and I'll feel for the first time the raspy, cold skin that will be close to me so many times in the future, it will be an odd feeling, not unpleasant, just odd, when before everything around me pulsated and gurgled, and now suddenly this. And he'll say something to me, but I won't understand what he's saying.

Papa. Papa. This is the way it's going to be, Papa. You'll come into my life, you'll be in it, and I'll devote a lot of time and effort to figuring out your stories. Stories from the old days without me, from a time when you couldn't accept a candy from a stranger in the street because it was poisoned for sure.

Translated by TAMARA M. SOBAN

ANDREJ BLATNIK

The Surface

ANDREJ BLATNIK

they park by the side of the road and the man looks at the car, worried about whether or not he has parked far enough onto the shoulder. Horrific images flicker through his mind: some careless driver grazing it in passing! He glances at the car keys in his hand, considers getting behind the wheel again, and redoing what's already done, but he can't bring himself to do it. If he did, the woman's lips would set into a thin, slightly quivering, disdainful line. You don't know how to do anything right, the familiar sneer would be saying; you can't do anything right the first time without having to correct it later.

The woman helps the child squirm out of his baby seat, then she takes the cloth-covered basket in which she's neatly, meticulously, thoughtfully packed a lunch, exactly by the book, for a Sunday family outing. The man pretends to be rapturously inhaling the fresh smell of ripe grasses, while he secretly measures the position of the car until the woman points out with unmasked irritation that the child has run on ahead and he'll have to follow him.

The grass is tall, luxuriant, dark green almost, and striding through it the man has to admit it does not smell as particularly fresh as he first thought; rather, it wafts a heavy, almost choking odor. As the little boy runs through the grass, the man can see him only from the waist up. He increases his pace, then realizes he won't catch up with the child this way. He shouts for him to stop, but the little boy only giggles and waves his arms in the air. The man wavers, glances back toward his car, and there sees his wife gesturing for him to hurry up; so he breaks into a trot.

The boy suddenly, totteringly, stops dead in his tracks. The man rapidly approaches him. He's just a few paces away when he sees that the child is standing on the very edge of a canal crossing a meadow that was previously concealed from sight by the grass. The little one teeters on the edge of the bank, turns his head to look at his father with huge, frightened eyes. Then he is pulled down by his own weight, down over the edge.

Springing forward with all his body, the man covers the few remaining paces in a single bound—he's on the edge, he throws himself into the emptiness, leaping after his child. Only when the murky, muddy water reeking of rot envelops him does he remember: he can't swim. But now, now that is irrelevant. Being the heavier of the two, he sinks faster and deeper than the child. He feels around for him underwater, grips him around the waist, and starts kicking as hard as he can. That's how swimming's done, he feels. That's what he tries, having no alternative.

His shoes slip off his feet and sink into the dark abyss beneath. The man feels that it's taking a very long time, too long, that they aren't moving at all, that they'll never come up to the surface. At the same time he thinks, in the strangely compressed time that has stopped in his head, that they can't have been underwater for very long since the air he breathed in just before breaking the surface still has not diminished, his lungs still feel pretty full.

Eventually he kicks his way up to the surface and pulls out his son. The child spews out a jet of putrid water and bursts into tears. The man feels the urge to hug the child close, even tighter, to just hold him and ignore everything else, absolutely everything in the whole world; then he feels the force pulling him back down and starts kicking again.

The woman is stretching her arms from the bank, and the man notices with astonishment that for the first time in all these years he can read confusion in her face, uncertainty, admission that the world has surprised her, proven to her that there are times when she cannot lay down the law. He hands over the child to her: suddenly the little fellow is light as a feather, weightless, like when he was newborn. And just like then, when he held him in his arms for the first time, still wet with birth water, the child feels soft and willing to belong to him completely, all of him. The woman puts him down next to her and the little boy immediately hugs her thigh, worriedly watching his father, who is trying to find, among the rocks lining the canal, a handhold to pull himself out onto the bank.

Finally, he succeeds and he drags himself up, his face so close to the dirt that he can see the tiny pores, the furrows made by ants, worms, and all kinds of minute creatures, so close that grit gets in his nostrils. He straightens up and attempts to smooth out, wipe clean his rumpled, soaking, filthy clothes. Then he realizes: this gesture is ridiculous. He stops doing it, and his arms float in the air in a strange, uncontrolled way. He looks at them flail, and thinks: Funny. Funny.

"How are you?" he asks the child. The child looks at him gravely. "Okay," he says. "Okay. I was scared I'd keep going down there. In there." The child presses to him. The man can smell the mud and the silt in the child's hair, and he signals to the woman to hand him the cloth covering the basket. Slowly and gently he dries his son's hair, and the boy looks at him unblinkingly while drops of water slide down his cheeks. They leave a wet trail, muddy on the edges.

In the evening the man sits on the bench in the front yard and smokes. The woman brings out a tray. Tea steams in the cups. "The little one's asleep," she says as she touches her husband's cheek.

The man ponders her action. He thinks about the expression he saw on her face when his son and he had surfaced. I won't let you get to me any more, he thinks. Now I know: we're equal. Equal. Neither of us knows how. You can't hide that from me anymore.

I'll quit my job, he thinks. It's pointless. The paperwork's all the same. Life's too short. And I have to say how I feel. Tell her too. It can't go on like this forever. Something's got to give. Also because of the little one. He could've well kept going there. In there. And I after him. We could've stayed down there. But we didn't. We came out. And now we're staying here. On the surface. I'm not going to let you get to me any more, no way.

He flicks the half-smoked cigarette in the air and follows it with his eyes. The last one, he says to himself. The last one. The glowing dot hovers above him for a second, then takes a nose dive and goes out. The man feels the open dome of the sky descending, embracing him, he senses the universe closing in. He smells the brittle trail of comets, the gravity of distant worlds brushes his cheek. Galaxies open up and beckon him in. The man knows: This is the beginning now; this is just the beginning.

Translated by TAMARA M. SOBAN

ANDREJ BLATNIK

It's a Good Thing Too

ANDREJ BLATNIK

Thanks for the melody, —SD

a man comes home from work, comes home a tad early and finds his wife in bed. With his best friend, needless to say. Wow, you're really going at it, aren't you?! What do I do now? What is it you're supposed to do exactly when something like this happens? he asks them, he's unprepared and all. Of course, right away it comes to him: in the closet under the shirts, wrapped in an old under-shirt, he's got some kind of gun or something. When the army went south, guns were cheap, so he thought he'd get himself a bit of a supply for a rainy day, like everybody who had a chance did.

Not a peep out of the two of them, sullen and tucked together under the sheets with delicate little flowers. He doesn't know the answer either. Why is it modern life has to be so convoluted? he thinks. He takes the gun out of the closet, like that, to make it clear what it is you have to figure with if you flout wedlock and go lying in the same bed. The wife says, Stop showing off, you won't do it, you don't have the guts, you're not that kind of macho. Oh, I'm not? the guy asks. Oh, I'm not? The friend takes him a lot more seriously, he can tell the red splotches on his face are not just summer sun. Oh, I'm not? the man screams, his friend's fear hav-ing given him, just in time, the courage he badly needs. Oh, I'm not?

He gets a good grip on the gun and sticks it under his friend's chin first and then under his own. The beads of sweat trickling down his friend's face drip onto the pistol, and the man doesn't like that at all, there's less and less dignity to the scene. Which is why he keeps shifting the pistol from under the other's chin to under his own, back and forth, faster and faster. All right, he yells at his wife, you tell us which one you love more, you decide which one I pop. She says to him two more times that he's really not the kind of man he's pretending to be; each time her voice is a little softer, and then she asks him nicely to please put the gun away. Or else she's calling the cops.

You call them, just you call them! the man tells her. Before you hang up, we'll all be dead, and by the time the cops arrive the house'll be burning too. He doesn't mean it, he's just threatening, for show, to terrify them and to get some of his confidence back. So what do people do when this happens to them? he asks himself again. How's he supposed to know that nobody goes around talking about these things? Whatever, violence doesn't seem to be in order, by nature he's the quiet sort, besides he did see that, despite everything, just like always, dinner is waiting for him in the kitchen, a nicely roasted bird in the oven reminds him that his woman isn't as bad as current conditions suggest.

He could have sworn the damn thing went off by itself somewhere halfway between his own neck and his friend's, and the bullet? Straight into the TV. A terrible bang and then dead silence. Not even the wife screams, the way you'd expect her to, no, they're all just listening to see what will happen now, who'll be the first to come hammering on the door. But nothing happens. Just more dead silence. As if nobody heard.

Then the wife softly says, And here I thought we were finally going to get to know our neighbors, and she laughs out loud. The friend starts looking around and the man understands why he's fidgeting and he tells him to get dressed, what if the cops do come, he can't meet the cops bare-ass like that, not to worry, with the wife you can finish some other time. The friend nods, begins pulling his pants on, and asks the husband if he knows how much he's shaking. I guess I really am, the husband thinks to himself, the way I am I couldn't even hit myself even if I wanted to, and anyways what am I doing with a gun, that's not my style. And he carefully wraps it back in his undershirt, and he puts it in front

ANDREJ BLATNIK

of him on the table, just so it's clear to everyone who the boss is. His mouth is dry, he feels that a beer would go nicely, he steps into the kitchen, goes to the fridge, but there's no beer.

The man asks his wife where the hell all his beer went to. The friend coughs and says could he maybe forgive him, the day was hot and everything, what're you going to do, and besides you know how I am, you know how when it comes to drink I have a hard time stopping once I start. To make up for it, he says, if they go across the street, it'll be his treat. The wife says she wants to come too, and so the three of them go and have one round, and then another.

When they've had quite a few and it's time to lock up and the waitress is pulling the chairs out from under their behinds, the man says to his friend, So, take my wife with you, okay, and I'm sorry I frightened you, forgive my selfishness, I hope you'll be very happy together, and if you ever have any extra money, you'll buy me a new TV and we'll be square. He knows he sounds a little teary-eyed, but what if he does, he thinks to himself, it's straight from the heart.

And his friend says, No, you take her home with you, she's yours after all, but first hit me. That's it, hit me, break my nose and tell me I'm a bastard. And if that's not good enough, you know where I live, I bet my wife doesn't keep her legs locked tight all these afternoons. And the wife says, even before the friend finishes because it looks like there's a real man-to-man talk starting to happen, the wife says, Don't fight over me, I don't deserve either of you, I should probably throw myself under a train or something, but life has its beautiful moments too and I'd hate to miss any of them, I've missed too many already, you both understand, right. . . . Anyway, you understand.

It's true, says the man, actually we've got a bird at home, that sort of thing is easy to heat up, why don't we all go to our place, I haven't eaten all day. Me neither, me neither, the other two agree, and they cajole one more round out of the waitress and then they go home for the bird. So you're not going to kick the shit out of me? the friend asks. They're gnawing on the last of the bones, pitching them over their shoulders onto the shards of glass on the floor as the sharp edges pleasantly mellow and the sight of the TV's pulverized maw starts to feel homier and homier. The man waves him off, it's not even worth mentioning. Are we friends or are we friends?

Then I guess I'll be going home, the friend says, is it late or what, my wife'll be worried, I'm the reliable sort, the type you can set your clock to. You can't drive a car drunk like you are, the man scolds him, you're sleeping here, life is too precious, you can't be toying with it like that. You're right, says the friend, you're right, where do I sleep? Sorry, he excuses himself, don't take it the wrong way, I didn't mean it like that.

The man is silent, he looks at his wife. She's silent too. How long has this been going on anyway? the man asks. The wife is still silent. You don't really want to know, right? she finally says. Anyways, you know that life really is a kind of operetta. Why should we pretend, what we all keep striving for is not to have it end before we've even noticed. So that somehow.... You know, you know what I mean: somehow.

I don't understand, the friend says, what is this crap you're talking about, do the two of you always talk like this? Forgive me, I'm very tired, I'll sleep right here. And he lies down on the couch in the living room, and right away he's snoring.

Wife, the man says, your chicken gets better every time, but did I really deserve this? Look at him, he didn't even take his shoes off. That's the kind of guy I catch you with? Excuse me, the wife says, he's your friend, you brought him into the house, you should have been choosier. Me, sad to say, I don't have a lot of opportunities to meet men. My life, you know, is not exactly the way I imagined it would be. And what should I do, you want me to cry over it in secret? You know how it is, we all do what we can. And, forgive me, I'm a little tired too, it's been a hard day. Why don't we go to bed? You've got to go to work tomorrow, remember?

And so they go into the bedroom and lie down, and just like every night the two of them hold hands. The man looks at the sheets and says,

ANDREJ BLATNIK

These little flowers, I don't like them, this we're gonna have to change. The wife murmurs something indistinct, strokes his hand, and falls asleep just like that, tired from the long day, but the man keeps looking at the ceiling for a long time yet, and in his mouth he can feel the salty taste of the nicely roasted chicken skin, and he thinks that maybe he paid too much for the gun and that maybe he can find somebody who would take it in exchange for a really good TV. Tomorrow, he thinks, he'll ask his friend if he knows somebody who might. There must be somebody who could use something like that, what with the times growing more unreliable every day. It's a good thing the guy down there snoring on his couch who didn't even take his shoes off is his friend, he thinks, as sleep overtakes him. Somebody else he might really have shot, and then everything would have been a lot weightier than he would have wanted it to be, and then there would have been no turning back. It's a good thing.

Translated by TOM LOZAR

Like Shit He Will

MOHOR HUDEJ

> He was human, but not fit to be among people!
> —BORUT KRAMER

"Hang in there," my dad said to me when I was going in to the management offices of the firm where from then on I'd be working as a sales assistant. I was going there to settle the final details concerning certain formalities the accountant was to explain to me. The financial arrangements, I presumed. I was as good as hired, and my father's ritualistic words of support were just a consequence of the fight we'd had, and of the annoyance and disappointment I had been for him and to Mom. I had screwed up another year at university. The troubled family relations had to be patched up somehow, and my father simply said something to make things right.

I nodded in response to his dramatic expectations, to the suspense that did not exist, since I had explained already at home that I had been hired. At first he had even wanted to come into the office with me, but I finally managed to sway him.

"I'm going in alone," I said, looking at him reproachfully.

"Alone?"

"I'm not five any more, fuck it!"

"Have it your way, then. Just don't blame it on me if it doesn't work out," he said, pretending to be hurt; his "Hang in there," then, was also meant for my courage in this sense.

"Oh? Good morning," I was greeted by the director when I entered his office. Also by two other managers, heads of two other branches of the firm, with whom I wouldn't have any contact. Mostly good bosses, who'd cause no problems. At least that was the impression I got. They seemed busy with something important and wanted to be rid of me as quickly as possible.

"Let me call Manca," the director said and dialed an extension. The other two pored over some papers in front of them, following something one of them pointed out with his forefinger.

"Manca, we've got that candidate here. Would Madame deign to honor us with her presence?" said the director jocularly into the phone. He liked to be informal in his dealings with employees. The more relaxed he was, the more easygoing his tone, and the more easygoing his tone, the heftier his bank account. I could have calculated what he was worth.

"She'll be right over. Take a seat for a moment," he said when he hung up.

And in came Madame Manca, a smile on her face. Apparently from having been touched by the director's affectionate tone. Behind this temporary emotion her true character shone through, her personal, permanent image. Ms. Chief Accountant from head to toe; the right measure of conceit and financial acumen, leaking into her broad smile and her crow's feet.

"As if we're in Japan, fuck it. A geisha," I thought.

The fundamental nature of her being an accountant had condensed and broken out in a pimple on the bridge of her nose, exactly on the spot where I had twice fractured mine.

When she entered I greeted her pleasantly.

"Good morning, Mrs. Vresnik!" I knew her last name from speaking to her on the phone the day before.

"Mrs. Presnik, if you don't mind. For the last twenty-five years," she said in a way that made the men smirk and then snicker. An internal joke. Beware of the Turks!

"Oh, is that so?" I was trying to be polite, at least.

"Follow me, then, we don't waste time around here. You know the old saying about time, don't you?" But she never told me. There was no time. A good accountant, no doubt.

"Be quiet!" I admonished myself. "Only speak if she asks you something."

I followed her down the hall and down the stairs to her office. She teetered along the brink. The brink separating a whole leg from a broken one. Far too confidently for her age. Her high heels struck the brink impudently and flexibly bounced back into a natural position. Undoubtedly, a good accountant.

Unpleasant, these interviews. They are vivid reminders of all those times when you have been confronted by a superior force, incapable of thinking of something clever to say that would go down well with the person across the desk, incapable even of using your instinctive charm, when you know it doesn't matter whether someone likes you or not, when you're made only in God's image (naïveté, being in love).

Again, I felt overwhelmingly like the little moron who doesn't have a clue about organic and inorganic substances, who just stares at the chemistry teacher, and can only hear his own shamefully impotent voice crying through her caustic voice:

"How can she be so mean, she's got kids too?"

Then the complex goes further:

"But her kids know what organic and inorganic substances are."

That made me think of the children of Madame the accountant.

"Look at you standing there," she said, relaxed. "Have a seat!"

She was searching for something on her computer when I sat down. She moved her lip to the left and bit on it. Her lower lip.

"I find it strange, though," she said and began to bite her lip again. I should have shown interest in what she found strange, but I didn't.

"Luckily or not?" I thought.

"I find it strange that you, being so young …" She now indicated which direction my thoughts should take and fell silent again.

"Say something," I urged myself, without coming up with any words that would make the conversation flow. The silence gave me the courage to answer her question with gravity.

She asked, "I wonder why you would like to become a sales assistant. Why would you like to sell jeans?"

"Why not?" I answered this totally inappropriate question. Who said anything about *liking to*? Would they *like to*?

"Wouldn't it be better if you chose something else for the time you're not enrolled at university, something more in keeping with your studies?"

"One's got to make a living, and this work pays well. There's no money in culture; well, there is some, but I'm a nobody … for now," I added, lest she gather the impression I had no ambition. People without ambition don't work well.

"That's true, sadly," she said upon my mention of culture, and now her tone provided insight into her bank account. She continued to look at me. I hadn't said enough. These sad things take longer. Instead of saying anything, I made some kind of stupid face, nodding to something.

When she grew tired of that, she said with some animation, "What did you say you study?"

"Comparative literature."

"That's like Slavic Studies?"

"Something along those lines, more like world literature. The other field is just languages. Sort of."

"What do you mean—sort of? Be a bit more specific, if you would. Nowadays, the right kind of information is worth a lot. I seek information everywhere, about everything, you know." She was instructing me, no doubt a good accountant.

Thus you fall prey to the greatest misfortune of all. That of becoming a source of information. Speaking about this is too painful and too serious, in the sense that infinity is serious.

I said, "It's like this, for instance: you take two authors, one Russian and one French, who both lived at approximately the same time. Say, both of them Romantics ..."

"'Like Prešeren ...?"

"Like Prešeren. And then you check out the motif of death in both their works, or something like that."

"What do you mean—the motif of death?"

"Well, if they believe in an afterlife, if there's Christian ethos, that's to say, if their eschatology is Christian, if we can talk of eschatology at all, and similar stuff."

"Uh-huh, uh-huh, I see. And who is, tell me, the greatest author, in your opinion?"

"Prežihov Voranc," I let slip out with a grin, cheeky bastard.

"Is that so? Well, you're the first one I've heard say that."

"I read him differently. I'm so into it, I'm only interested in details, and these are often of a very speculative nature."

I scared her with all this mighty information, the good Mrs. Presnik. And that doesn't really suit an accountant. She was a good accountant, and with sensibility she reverted to more solid ground.

"Well, whatever. I can see you're a smart young man, but selling jeans bears no relation to *Anna Karenina* or *The Brothers Karamazov*."

A lady with good taste, no doubt. And a smile to testify to that.

"I'm aware of that. I'll work hard," I said.

"The figures must add up!"

"Mine will."

"There are three of you. All your figures must add up! There's no me/you/him! You're all one!"

"Yes, well ... I mean, it's hard to say anything now. I don't mean to imply any distrust beforehand.... But, I can hardly speak for the others."

They were obviously used to having the greatest fuck-ups in departments where it's everyone for themselves. She gave me a dark look that said, "Watch out, boy, it's not a wrap yet!"

When she saw I had understood—she put great score by her "psychological" sense—she continued.

"It's no good passing the buck; we're all in this together. One team. Everyone does their bit, contributes their part. Every drop of this energy is a link in our structure. We all sow, we all reap. That's the thing to remember!"

"Yes ma'am."

I'd been taught to say something similar in the army, and now it came in handy. No room left for screwing around.

She calmed down; her eyes lost their faraway look. There seemed nothing for me to fear any more. She took my worker's booklet and the report from my physical declaring me fit for the job. The conditions had been met, I had successfully passed all the tests, she could sum up:

"You know, you might've thought it was the director who decided your fate, but I'll have you know I'm the one who has the final say in this. I can see here you're a healthy person, you have a vision, you'll work for the good of the company first, and only then for your own benefit," she smirked. "The job you'll be doing is a good one; one of the better jobs we've offered lately. Don't forget that. You've got what it takes. University gave you that, I can tell you've done a lot of reading, you have good communication skills, you can speak well. Which year are you in at university?"

"I should've finished my final year and be writing my thesis now, but I was a bit lazy," I said in a voice that knew what it was saying, that regretted the mistake it had made and that would mend its ways.

She wasn't listening. She was already writing on my worker's booklet and she said, "Good-bye for now. This is your first day of work. We'll be in touch more often from now on. Don't forget you've got a good job."

"I won't," I said idiotically, and we parted company by the book.

"Did you get it? Did you?" asked my father, already opening the car door for me as I came out.

"I did," I told him. He was as delighted as a child, and some of his joy rubbed off on me.

"Tell me about it," he said as he pulled out into the traffic.

"What do you want me to tell you?"

"The things they said to you."

"They said ... Actually, *she* said. I only spoke to the accountant. She said I was hired."

"I know that, what else did she say?"

"I don't know, I don't remember...."

"What do you mean you don't know? You don't kid around with an accountant. Sometimes they have more to say than the director."

I reflected.

"She asked me who the greatest author was."

"You didn't start philosophizing, did you?"

"No, I didn't."

"What did you say? She didn't ask you just like that, you know, pointlessly. They're cunning. Psychologically cunning. She must be a good accountant, that one. She's analyzed you to the core. It's best to say exactly what you'd said to the director. They all discuss these things behind your back. Did you tell her what you told the director?"

"I did." It wouldn't have made any sense to tell him anything other than this simple lie.

We fell silent for a while, then my father continued didactically, "I've been thinking.... I don't mean to teach you your business, but you must realize you're not hired yet! Not yet! Do you understand? This is only the beginning. You have to earn such a good job. Now the practical tests start: They'll put sums of money in your way, and surplus material, they'll send undercover agents, people who work for them, to get you to cash checks and do stuff like that.... Don't fall for any of that, don't trust anyone. Be honest and proud. That always works best. Then you can get your driver's license and become a sales rep, and then you can actually afford quite a few of the things you'll be offered as bait. For now, though, there's only honesty. Don't think the boss won't notice. It'll give you power!"

"Power?"

"Yes, power," he said and then we were silent again, all the way home, where he said, still outside the house, "A good job. You landed a good one. You landed it, ha-ha."

Lunch was ready and waiting. Mom had already started. She looked up from her soup and asked, "What now?"

"What do you mean—what now?"

"Have they hired you?"

"They'd already hired me last time; today was just a formality."

She nodded into her plate. We fell silent. Dad murmured something and cleared his throat.

The annoyance got on my nerves. Mom resented the fact that I'd be a salesman. She could picture me teaching literature; she was a teacher herself.

"So you're just where you wanted to be," she said.

"I don't give a fuck," I said. Normally, I didn't swear at home.

"You don't, do you. . . . I can see that," she said nervously. She wasn't used to my swearing at home.

I made a farting noise with my mouth.

"You know best, seeing as you're so smart," she said.

"I do," I said, knowing I shouldn't have.

"Like shit you do," she said.

"He'll know best, all right. It's a good job," my dad said.

"Like shit he will," my mom refused to hear the part about the job being good.

"I don't give a fuck," I reiterated my previous thought.

"I can see that," Mom reiterated her previous thought.

"Don't start a fight," Dad said, surprisingly. "It's not a bad job."

"Like shit it isn't," said Mom, rising to her feet and off to the sink to start doing the dishes.

"It's a lousy job," I rose and left.

I heard my dad say to my mom, "He'll finish university all right. The lad did well at the interview."

"Like shit he will." Mom ignored the bit about my having done well at the interview.

Translated by TAMARA M. SOBAN

Like My Brother

MIHA MAZZINI

there's not much to say about my life. I'm forty years old, have never married and have no children. I've had a few girlfriends, but they never lasted long because of my responsibilities; in recent years I've stopped even trying. My parents had me quite late: my mother was thirty-six, my father two years older. I've read that these days women want to give birth as late as possible and doctors accommodate them, but in those days having a child that late was rather an exception. They've never actually said anything, but I was fully aware that I was a replacement for their first son who died at the age of fourteen, a year before I was born. He was run over by a car crossing the road; I don't know the details. Not one item belonging to him remained. Once I secretly searched all the wardrobes and cupboards in the apartment and couldn't find a single photograph of him. When I quietly closed the last drawer, I was overcome by a deep gratitude to my parents. How bravely they were trying to leave the past behind them and provide me with a clear beginning. A futile effort; their sadness remained and roamed the small, one-bedroom apartment like a ghost. They stopped going to work after my brother's death, we lived on welfare, and they spent the largest part of the day in bed. Bottles full of cigarette butts accumulated beside them, and the television remained on all night. They moved slowly—it seemed to me as if they were shut into a world of their own to which I had no access. I remember they occasionally spoke about my brother when I was still young, but later there were just beginnings of sentences, such as "Your brother ..." or "Your brother would ...," and then their lips would compress and their eyes would melt with sadness.

Finally, they stopped mentioning him at all, but I knew that they were constantly comparing me to him. Whatever I said or did, I always thought of how he would have acted; I believed that he would be able to get my mother and father to smile again, and I felt stupid and useless.

Time didn't heal my parents' wounds. I couldn't leave them alone. After the first year of economics school, I took a job at a factory and completed my secondary education in the evenings. I gave all the money I earned to my mother, and when she died five years ago from a woman's condition—or so my father told me, he never let me visit her in the hospital, saying it would upset me too much—I started taking care of everything myself.

My father successfully hid his feelings at my mother's death. Or perhaps a man who has not yet gotten over the loss of his son can't be damaged any further by the death of his spouse. But I would see his eyes become even more filled with pain. My schoolmates and neighbors used to say what an admirable couple they had been. They had found each other when they were eighteen and remained together their whole life. They said I was lucky to have them, and my chest swelled with pride. In today's world full of divorce and evasion of responsibility, they really were exceptional.

When I finished my degree, I was promoted to an office position. The work is not that interesting: I receive data about materials and then copy the numbers from the blue sheets into the first column, from the red sheets into the second column, and from the yellow sheets into the third. But the job leaves me with enough time to cook lunch and dinner and do everything needed to ease my father's old age.

During the rare moments when I'm alone and my father doesn't need me, I turn on the radio and, using earphones so as not to disturb or wake him, I listen to the classical music station. I don't know anything about music, but it feels as if the violins are stroking me as I stare out of the window. When opera comes on, I turn the dial.

"I won't be around much longer," father said to me yesterday when I went to visit him at the hospital after work. I sat on the edge of his bed, hiding him with my body so that I could tip the small bottle of brandy he'd requested into his mouth. He grabbed my wrists, and all I could feel were bones enveloped in skin. The drink nearly suffocated him, but when he caught his breath, he thanked me. "That's just what I needed!"

He gestured toward the open door.

"I can see what they're thinking. Last night the duty nurses thought I was asleep and talked a bit too loud."

I hid the bottle in my pocket. I did not know what to say to him, so we remained silent. I felt like crying when I looked at his skull-like face, the yellowed eyes, and the few grey hairs getting creased between the crown of his head and the pillow. Tubes led from both his arms, and the two bottles on the stand slowly dripped into them.

"I'd do anything for a cigarette!" he said and gave me a mournful look.

"Father . . ."

I couldn't oblige. When I let him persuade me on my first visit, I was immediately caught by the nurse who scolded me and asked me to leave. She threatened that they wouldn't let me visit him any more. In spite of this, I felt guilty and couldn't bear his eyes. So I stared down at the floor.

"I know," he said after a while, and I was able to lift my head again.

"We come, we are, we depart," he said lightly. "That's how it is, and there's nothing we can do about it. The only thing we can aim for is for it to pass as comfortably as possible."

I reached out to adjust his pillow, but his eyes stopped me. He stared at me, not through me as he usually did. There was a strange, unfamiliar sparkle in his eyes.

"You always did well at school, didn't you? Not at first, though. In the early years, when you started elementary school, you barely just got by, but then you started getting good grades and never stopped. Remember?"

I nodded.

They had removed his dentures, and it was an effort to understand him. His cheeks had sunk and were flapping against the few remaining yellow teeth still barely attached to his gums. A wide pink hole gaped out of his front. I remembered his stomach, and how I had always wanted to press myself against it when I was still a child. Now there were only bones left, deep-seated wrinkles, and a week's worth of stubble on his cheeks.

"Do you remember when we had money troubles and your mother got a job delivering papers?"

I nodded again.

"She was supposed to get up at five in the morning and deliver them on her bike. But you volunteered to do it instead of her every day before school. She never had to go out once."

He was looking at me as if he was expecting something from me. I became embarrassed, so I looked at the tips of my shoes and then at the two metal dishes sitting beneath the bedside cabinet. The nurses called them kidney dishes.

We remained silent.

"Do you remember what fun we had when there was that terrible flu going around and you went to the butcher's to get us a pound of beef and then made us some soup?"

I nodded.

"We were all feverish, with a temperature of over a hundred, but you kept making that soup, and then you poured it into the tureen on the table? Do you remember?"

I didn't know why of all the memories we shared he had to recall one that was most unpleasant to me. Why was he asking me these strange questions? Was he losing his mind?

"Then you put a chair on each side of the bed, so that we could eat, and you went to get the soup. Do you remember? That was a fun time, wasn't it?"

I nodded.

"How we laughed! It was fun, wasn't it?"

While I was in the kitchen, father secretly Super-glued the tureen to the table. I still have a scar on my right leg from the soup spilling over it as I lifted the tureen too quickly and the table along with it.

"Come on, admit it, we knew how to have fun, didn't we?"

I nodded.

My father withdrew his eyes and slowly turned his head toward the window. The tops of pine trees and the mountains in the distance could be seen from the third floor. One of the other two patients in the room started coughing behind my back, and my father said nothing until the noise had stopped. He had always had a strange sense of humor, and although it's a sin to say it, I didn't like his jokes. Some days before school I would have to search in panic for my notebooks that he had hidden. Sometimes I would step into a puddle of sticky liquid he had put on the floor, or I would use the wrong spice when cooking because my father had switched the contents. Years ago I had come to the conclusion that these clumsy pranks were probably the only ways in which he was able to express his feelings for me. He could not and would not do it in any other way.

"So I said to myself last night after I'd heard the nurses, why not have some more fun before I depart from this world? A good laugh is as good as a good rest, isn't it?"

He was staring straight at me.

"Tell me how you felt."

I said nothing.

"Well, how did you feel? I don't really know anything about school, but how did you feel when you were delivering the papers? And that time with the soup?"

I was so surprised with this line of questioning that I didn't even look away any more.

"Oh, go on, tell me, I won't be around much longer."

I closed my eyes and asked myself why I felt as if I would burst into tears at any moment. True, I was sitting at the bedside of a dying person, but it was a completely different kind of crying that was arising in me. I didn't dare think what kind it was.

"Don't then," father sounded disappointed. "Obviously I'll have to do all the talking."

I raised his head near to the glass so that he could take a sip of water to moisten his lips, some of it trickling down his neck. I wiped it off with a muslin cloth he had stashed under his pillow.

After a long silence, he started talking evenly, without taking his eyes off me for a moment.

"Ah," he went on, "why am I telling you this? You were there. Why don't you tell me instead what all these memories have in common?"

I didn't understand.

"The soup, the papers, the school?"

I shook my head.

"You really don't remember? Come on, you've always been a clever boy."

I felt small and stupid. I blushed and looked at the floor. I so much wanted not to disappoint him even on his deathbed, but my head was completely empty and I couldn't find a single word.

"Why did you make the soup? Why did you go delivering newspapers? Why did you start doing better at school? Because . . ."

I answered, but I don't know where the words had come from. They just slipped out of me:

"Because my brother would have done it."

"There, you see, you can do it."

Father breathed a sigh of relief. He ran his dry tongue over his parched lips, and I helped him to take another drink.

The feeling that I would cry, which had begun to subside, was growing again. My brother ... I remembered all my attempts to show that I was as capable and good as he had been, and that my parents could be proud of me. I imagined him blond (my hair was black), always smiling (I was constantly worried and on guard as to when I would have to prove myself again and in fear that I would fail), clever (my words always seemed somehow hollow, and I thought my parents were always exchanging secret and pitying looks on hearing them). In a word, he was the exact opposite of me in everything, and therefore I could never be like him.

"How did you feel?"

This time it came to me, but I didn't want to answer. It wouldn't be fair to a dying man. I looked at the floor again.

"Go on, tell me! I've always wanted to know. I'd like to know if I was right."

I shook my head.

He sighed.

He made a funny gargling noise, like steam being released from a radiator. I was frightened that this was his last breath. When I looked at him, he was pressing his lips firmly together and his eyes were bulging.

"Father!"

I jumped up, wanting to pull the alarm cord, but he stopped me with his hand so that the drip bottle swayed.

I sat down uncertainly again and waited for his breathing to settle. His lower lip was curled between his two remaining back teeth, and he was biting it. He was shaking in waves from head to toe.

"Father, are you in pain? I'll get the nurse...."

I started to get up when he gestured to me again. I slowly sat back down and watched him try to control the pain. Eventually he opened his mouth wide, exhaled with a weak whistle, and stared at the ceiling for a while, before turning toward me again.

"Your mother and I had a good life. I'm not complaining. You switch on the television and you see people slaughtering each other, slaving away in stupid jobs, doing all sorts of silly things, while we lived in peace. We had a drink or two and a lie-down and our lives went by. I don't know quite what happened, but when your mother realized she was pregnant, it was too late for an abortion. Anyway, we said an abortion was also a lot of effort, so we'd just keep the baby. And then you were born. A child means nothing but more work and struggle. You can't even imagine how lucky you are not to have any. It's . . ."

He waved his hand feebly and continued.

"A difficult job—what can I say? We couldn't have done it on our own. . . ."

He shook his head and stopped talking.

A wind started up outside and the tree branches swished. The brown leaves flew past in a swarm. Father turned toward the window and we both looked outside for a while.

"We needed help," he said when he turned back to me again. "Oh, your brother! Your brother!"

He kept going on about my brother and then his cheeks puffed out, he sat up suddenly, and I supported him with my arm and held a kidney dish in front of him, but he overcame the urge to vomit and repeated a few more times: "Your brother, your brother."

Our faces were inches apart when he said, "He never existed."

"I know," I said. "He died."

I was holding him, still with that enameled dish beneath his chin and his head shaking on my forearm.

"No, he was never born. He didn't exist. But your mother and I needed help. Bringing up a child is a difficult matter! At first, we used to leave you on your own. We hardly even fed you, but you somehow managed to stay around. But then, seeing how obstinate you were, we decided to use you. It was your mother's idea. Once she said, 'Wouldn't it be grand if he had an older brother to look after him?' And so it started. I objected a bit at first, but then she said, 'If priests can do it, why can't we?' And she was right. Everything became simpler after that.

In the end, all we had to do was say, 'Your brother would go and make us some soup,' or 'Your brother would go and do your mother's work,' or 'Your brother had top grades at school,' and you immediately jumped. No difficulties, no effort whatsoever. In the end we didn't even have to say anything. We only had to give you a sad look, and you did everything. How well we'd trained you!"

His dull pupils floated in the middle of his yellow eyeballs.

"Why are you holding me like this? Let go of me! Do you think I'm going to throw up or something? Where do you get that idea?"

I was unable to move. I could now see the two of us, as if I was hovering above him. An old man, held by a bald man with glasses who looked far too old for his age, with patches on the elbows of his tatty cardigan. A trembling hand holding a kidney dish.

More air escaped from my father's insides, and this time I recognized it for what it was. He was trying to hold back his laughter.

"Hahahaha!!!!" escaped from him, and my arm moved away. Father fell back on his pillow and the pain interrupted his laughter, while I found myself back on the chair and in my body, although I was still able only to observe, not to move.

"Yes," he almost shouted, "tell me, how did you feel? How? How?"

The words escaped very quietly, but he still heard them.

"Like a dog."

Another outburst of air, another deformed laugh he could only barely suppress.

"I knew it, I knew it! Your mother and I kept wondering how long you'd last. We thought you'd realize, being such a clever boy. But no, there's something inside you, just like there is in those who run to church to grovel or go into politics. All the things we made you do, but you just kept coming back for more. What fun we had! We always liked a good joke. Those big eyes of yours, just like a dog's. If I'd told you that your brother had licked our shit, you'd have done that, too. You were lucky, really, that we couldn't be bothered to keep coming up with new ideas all the time, we were too lazy for that. Ha, ha, ha. And do you know why I'm telling you this now? Do you? Because I don't need you any more. Your mother's liver packed up, but do you know, she wanted to tell you, the silly cow! I said to her, 'Mother, don't be silly, you're finished with your life, why tell him now, so that I'll have to get through the rest of mine alone or what?' She promised to keep quiet, but I didn't trust her. Women go a bit peculiar when they're dying. So I didn't let you go to her, just in case. And I went to the bar instead, maybe visited her every other day or so, although sitting by a sickbed is also such an effort. Well, now it's my turn. This liver of mine. I'll be gone today or tomorrow, so I said to myself, 'Go on, have another laugh.' Ha, ha, ha. And you thought I was in pain, eh? Ha, ha, ha, ha! Got you! HA HA HA!"

His laughter grew louder and louder. He started waving his arms around, the bottles rattled on their stands, his body was jumping up and down and the metal frame of the bed joined it.

"HO HO HO HA HA HA AAAAAAARRRRGGGGG HO HE HA HO HO HO!!!!!"

His mouth opened wide, the tongue flapping against his palate and teeth. His saliva escaped in an arch over his gums, spraying me. He was howling with laughter, beating his stomach, the needles were swaying in the air, on one of them there were two plasters in the shape of an X, blood was spraying from the inside of his elbow.

"AHAHAHAHAHAHA!!!!!"

I could feel something rising in me. It reached my throat, and I thought that a shapeless black mass would emerge. That it would burst out and never stop. It would fill the room; father and the other two patients, everybody, everybody would suffocate beneath it. It would consume the world. I started swallowing like mad, I gulped and gulped, my father was laughing while I struggled with something black inside me, trying to push it back down, to the base of my stomach, back to where it came from. Suddenly a vicious pain tore at my insides, I bent over, pressing both hands on my stomach and fell off the chair and onto my knees. I struggled for air, and when I was able to breathe again, I knew my father was as good as dead, although he was still neighing with all his strength.

I got up and left. Two nurses came running past me in the corridor, they gave me a strange look, but they rushed on toward the laughter I was leaving behind.

I didn't go to work today. The phone rang a few times; I left it, there was nothing new they could tell me. Out of habit I put on my earphones, but the violins wouldn't caress me this time.

Memories slowly unwound in my head, all ending with my desperate desire for the love I wanted to earn. I was ashamed.

I took a sheet of paper and started making holes in it with the scissors, then with a ballpoint, and in the end I started writing. About my parents, about myself. I didn't dare stop, maybe I never will. I want to remember everything so that it never happens again, so that I don't overlook anything, so that I don't go blind again.

When I wrote my brother's name for the first time, I paused. I remembered my father teaching me how to swim. He dropped me in the swimming pool, the water engulfed me and I trembled with horror as I lay at the bottom of the pool, slowly losing consciousness. I was saved by the thought of my brother, who was an excellent swimmer. If he could do it … I pushed myself up and from that moment on I stopped being afraid of water.

I realized my brother had never existed anywhere but inside of me. I sat there repeating to myself: "In me … In me … In me …" There was something in this thought, something I did not quite comprehend yet, but I felt as if I was in that pool again, and that I was starting to feel that same force inside me that would help me rise to the surface again.

Translated by MAJA VISENJAK LIMON

Geographical Positions

SUZANA TRATNIK

Studying maps has always been a very dear and mysterious activity for me. The first secret is that one does not look at a map; one reads it.

At the international conference for lesbian and gay rights, I shared a room with Krisa from Fiji. Never before had I even thought about what people from that island, which is its own country, looked like. Krisa was thin, had somewhat darker skin and slightly slanted eyes. When I asked her the meaning of the drawings, apart from the sea motifs tattooed on her upper arm and forearm, she said they were Chinese characters. Her father was Chinese, her mother, Fijian. "If you think that the inhabitants of my island look like me, you are very mistaken," she explained to me. "They all have darker skin, more pronounced features, and their eyes are straight, almost like you Europeans."

Reading, of course, is something you learn at school. Then you read a map and have to make out north and south, east and west. Why north should be up isn't entirely obvious and it is in fact only "up" on the map. In reality, in outer space, up and down don't matter. But this is still okay. We know where south is, it's down after all and we all say that everyone "looks down" on southerners. According to this, we could "look up" to people from the north, but I'm not sure if it works this way or not. Okay, east and west—right and left. Right is east, that's where Russians and Communism are; left is west, where Americans and other capitalists are. You can try to remember it all like this: On the right are Communists, who are politically left-wing, on the left are capitalists, who are politically right-wing. This is more complicated, but I think it's easier to remember. Of course, this also depends on your current political situation. Nowadays left and right aren't what they used to be. It used to be much easier to read maps, when we weren't in transition. Just the fact that time has something to do with all this is enough—on some points on a map, it can be an hour later or earlier than somewhere else—especially if you're looking at it all from some sort of transition.

Before using logic, one has to learn a bunch of facts that don't seem to go together. It just doesn't seem logical that east is east, so one needs something else to remember its position. For example, that east is on the right side or that it is Communist or retarded or that it reeks of garlic (even Dracula, who was always chased away with garlic, comes from the east). It seems to you that you've been cheating while learning all these positions. I am sometimes worried about what my (geographical) logic is based on. I'm afraid that it's still based on cheating. If I hear that a certain place is in the east, of course I know where east is, but at the same time, I think to myself that I have to read the right side of the map. To the right of Europe.

Two days later when Krisa and I were embracing each other in bed, we first had to come to an agreement about geographical positions. She did not know where Slovenia was and asked me if English was our only official language. I told her that we spoke Slovene, but there really wasn't much point to that because she could only understand Slovenia as being a part of Europe—this was probably her way of cheating when learning about places outside of Oceania. Though, I wasn't much better; I wasn't able to place Fiji on that map in my head. I kept getting lost, I wasn't able to place it on the left nor the right. When I was back at home, I finally looked at a map of the world; I usually looked for Oceania on the right side. And so I began my search for Krisa's island. I looked to the extreme right and found Fiji. Then I looked to the extreme left and found Fiji there too!

Krisa had had more than enough of her island of Fiji. She wanted to go to America, to New York, San Francisco, anywhere. She knew very little about Europe, she said that this continent seemed too foreign. My explanations about Europe being called the Old World as opposed to America being called the New World were a waste of time. It seemed to her that she had once heard something about this, but my explanations were too abstract for her, perhaps even unreal. Krisa wanted to study in America. At home she worked for a nongovernmental organization for sexual minorities, which in the eyes of the locals was not worthy of respect. My Fijian roommate had many problems with respect in general. Now that she had finally gotten a job and moved into an apartment with her three children, everyone found out that she was a negligent lesbian, even though she herself categorized herself as bisexual. Before that she had been without her kids for some months because she'd left home. She left home because her brother had beaten her unconscious. He'd beaten her up because she had told him that a taxi driver had raped her. The taxi driver had raped her because her friend had gotten out of the taxi before her and Krisa had been left alone with the driver. They'd taken a taxi because they'd been going home very late at night, or morning rather, at six when it was still dark and too dangerous to go on foot. They had been so late because Krisa had been working as a DJ in a club where her friend was a waitress.

So, to the right and to the left of Europe—Fiji twice—at least to me. To Krisa there was no Slovenia and Fiji was probably only once. Surely, she doesn't read maps on the "left and right sides" of Europe. Europe is the center of the map to me, the point I don't search left or right for, nor up or down. This centered view of Europe pushes other territories to the extreme edges of paper maps. What about a round globe on which all are the same? Reading a globe isn't as pleasant to an eye that isn't used to it. Its center is somewhere else—there somewhere in hot lava, but no less geo/egocentric.

One evening after a busy day at the conference, three of us got together in the room and were drinking wine. Krisa combed her long hair in front of the mirror, Esthera from Latvia and I had wrapped ourselves in cigarette smoke.

"Then I remembered that it had begun even earlier," Krisa suddenly said in the bathroom.

Esthera and I looked at each other and waited for Krisa to go on. After the rape and her brother's beatings, she left home and left her kids with her mother. She was no longer able to work as a DJ; she rented a room and began to earn money as a prostitute.

"It's far from the best profession in the world," she said as she came out of the bathroom with combed shiny blue hair. "Yet I found it very informative."

She laughed sharply and the two of us joined her with careful smiles. We had noticed that she often laughed at inappropriate times. She sat down with us, drank some wine and then continued.

Most of the time, I probably still imagine the world in a primitive way, flat. My favorite cartographic projection.

Whenever I fly from one town to another, I never think about how much of the Earth's curved surface is below us. Distances on a flat map seem somewhat friendlier to me, shorter, easier to conquer.

While prostituting she realized that there had been others before the taxi driver. She had been raped by her older brother, the one who beat her up for getting raped. And before that by her uncle, who would never let her leave the table until she had eaten everything up. When her clients paid her for sex, she finally remembered why she had such unpleasant memories of that part of her childhood, which she had spent at her uncle's while her parents had been in China. Perhaps she had forgotten about it because she had known that she wouldn't have been able to tell anyone. Rather, no one would have believed her.

There are, of course, measurements for geographical coordinates. They are usually found in the lower right-hand corner of most maps.

"But sometimes it's possible," the Latvian said pensively. Krisa and I looked at her in surprise. "Sometimes it's possible," she continued, "for an adult to love a child. I mean: like a sexual object."

"But that's abuse," Krisa and I said in unison. "It is always abuse, everywhere. A child isn't responsible for himself, an adult is. A child doesn't have all the information, an adult knows what he or she is doing."

"I know," said the Latvian quietly. "But still. A child can also love an adult. You love and desire without information and responsibility. I'm only saying that it's possible."

A shadow of disappointment and rage covered Krisa's face as she drank up what was in her glass.

"Perhaps it's possible," she said with a blunt look centered at the hotel wallpaper above Esthera's head, "but that is deception. Manipulation."

"But love between two adults is never deceitful?" Esthera asked.

I shrugged. "I think that's too general a view."

"In any case, I don't know anything about love between adults and children," said Krisa as she laughed sharply. This time her laughter had cut the conversation. And all three of us silently tried to regain our balance on the slippery terrain on which we had found ourselves.

Without numbers that express ratios, one to so much and so many thousands, tens of thousands or hundreds of thousands, we'd find it hard to believe that we actually read anything on a map.

Then Krisa thought that we could still go for some champagne; it was, after all, our last evening together. We quickly got dressed and left the window open.

In the hotel lobby I looked at a local map. We were all at the same point: at 26 degrees south and 29 degrees east.

Translated by ELIZABETA ŽARGI and KELLY LENOX

Hansel and Gretel

POLONA GLAVAN

*Y*ou are so terribly cute, he says. You've got such lovely cheeks, and these eyes—I could eat you up, he says, tickling me under my chin. I'm laughing. I tell him he shouldn't eat me, that it hurts. He laughs and says he'll eat me anyway. I say I'll tell Daddy and he'll see. So what, little girl, he says. You won't care to do that. You'll already be in my stomach at the time, ha ha ha. He grasps me around my waist and rolls me over onto my back. Then he runs his fingers up and down and I'm screaming, trying to reach out for his hair. Little girl, little girl, he repeats, I don't care, I don't, no, no, and he keeps tickling me and I'm screaming until Mama comes running into the room. She's angry. I know it because her nose is white. Let go of her, Andrej, she says. Go and do your homework instead. Andrej puts his hands away and sits on the bed. He's quiet. It's better to be quiet when Mama's angry. I must be quiet too, though I'm small. The three of us are quiet until Mama nods her head and leaves the room. Andrej turns to me. He's smiling. Hush, he says putting finger on his lips. Mama has things to worry about. Yeah I know, I say, pulling him by the hair anyway. He grits his teeth but says nothing. Then he smiles again. It's alright, little girl, he says. Leave me alone for a while now, okay? I have to do my homework.

I nod my head and watch him sitting down at the desk. Andrej is already big. He says he was already going to school when I was still in my mama's tummy. Now I'm quite big, but not as big as Andrej. He knows a lot. He knows how to speak and write English. I already know almost all the letters and I can sign my name, though it's awfully long. It takes me a whole notebook line to write down ALEKSANDRA. But almost no one calls me this. Andrej always calls me little girl. He says I won't be able to spell it soon. He also says I have beautiful skin. His is full of red spots. Sometimes he's naughty. He hides my Barbie that Aunt Urša gave me for my birthday. Then I beat him with a pillow until he gives it back. But I never tell Mama. If I went to tell my mama, Andrej would call me a big mouth and he wouldn't love me anymore.

The other night Andrej came into my bed. He said he'd tell me a fairy tale. I said I want to hear the one about Hansel and Gretel. Alright, he said, so I'm gonna tell you this one. But then around the point where Hansel and Gretel come to the witch's house he suddenly got weird. He started looking at me funny and stroking me on the legs. I told him to keep telling me the story. Yes, he said, I will. After a couple of minutes he got quiet again. He was breathing aloud and started looking at me funny again. I asked if he felt sick. He shook his head. He stroked me on the belly. I said, What's up with you? Nothing's wrong with me, little girl. I love you. I want you to know that I love you more than anybody ever will. Do you love me too, little girl? I said I do. I'll marry you when I grow up, I said. He smiled. Fine, he said. He started breathing aloud again. Then he gave me a kiss. But not the one as usual. More weird. He pushed his tongue into my mouth. I didn't like it so I pushed him away. I said it was yuck. Okay, he said, nothing then. I'll do something else, Okay? I said, it's okay as long as it's not yuck. It won't be, he said. Because you're my little girl. Because I love you so much. I'll only do nice things to you because I want you to feel fine. Okay? Yes, I said. He was looking at me still, in that funny way again. Then he started shaking. Listen, he said. Be quiet completely. Only if it hurts you. If it hurts, tell me. Just don't scream, little girl. Then Mama will be angry again and it's not alright, is it? I nodded. It really isn't alright. Mama is angry all the time anyway. Close your eyes, said Andrej. He was stroking me on the belly and then lower. Little girl, he said, and then again, little girl. Then he started kissing me everywhere. It was tickling me in some strange way. I started laughing. Hush, said Andrej. Be quiet, little girl. Then he suddenly put something inside me. I wanted to ask him what it is. What he's doing. But the thing wasn't there anymore. I opened my eyes. Andrej was looking completely shattered. Did it hurt, he said. I said it didn't. I knew it, he said. He was like his old self again. He smiled. You're so brave, little girl. I knew it you wouldn't hurt. Only cowards hurt. Cowards and big mouths. But you're not like that, are you, little girl? You're my big brave sister!

I love it most when Andrej says I'm brave. Now he's saying this to me all the time. He was with me in my bed many times already. We do that thing almost every time. He says it's done by those who are in love, who really love each other. And he loves me. And I love him. When we're big, we'll get married. Now we can't yet, says Andrej. He says he'll never love any other girl as much as me. That he won't do it with any other girl. The other day Aunt Urša dropped by and she said to him that he looked like the hunchback of Notre Dame with that hair of his. I don't know what a hunchback of Notre Dame is. Andrej told me Aunt Urša meant to say he's got to have a haircut. That he'll look more good then. But he already looks good enough to me. He teaches me how to speak English. I can say I love you. He says I must say it to him. He says the same to me. Then he kisses me everywhere, on the feet too. It tickles, but I don't scream. I wanna be brave so he'll love me even more. Snowdrops are falling outside. I want to bring him some, but he'd probably laugh. I'd better bring them to Mama, for her day. Or to Grandma. Or to my nurse in the kindergarten, she's always so kind even when I'm arguing with someone. Once Andrej came to pick me up and she asked him if he had a girlfriend. She's my girlfriend, said Andrej and the nurse was laughing and said how beautiful it was. Then we laughed too. On the way back he bought me a piece of cake. He told me a tale he made up himself. It was about a little boy who caught a cloud and tied it on a string like a puppy. It was a bit sad in the end. I don't know if the cloud escaped or what. Maybe it just took a little boy along to the sky.

Now it's been completely different for a long time. I'm not laughing anymore. I don't remember everything that went on then. I only remember how the door tore open. It was Mama and her nose was all white. Then she was just standing and watching. At the end her whole face got white. Then she was screaming and screaming and Daddy ran there. I was scared so I started crying. Daddy jumped to Andrej and pulled him from under the cover by the hair. It was cold. I was scared. Mama was screaming and then I started screaming too. Finally Mama jumped on me and squeezed me so tight that it hurt. I started crying. I knew something terrible was about to happen. I pulled myself from Mama's lap and screamed I love you, Andrej! He didn't answer. I started crying very loud and I was crying until the doctor came and then there was nothing left there.

Now I haven't been to the kindergarten for the whole month. Mama's always home too. She keeps eating some pills. Aunt Urša is bringing me dolls and sweets. But I don't want anything. I want Andrej. He's gone away. Daddy says he went to some big house where boys like him are kept. Mama doesn't want to tell me anything. She's just asking if it hurt. Aunt Urša says it too, and Uncle Janez who's a doctor. I tell them it didn't. If it hurt I'd strike him anyway. I'm a brave little girl. I cry many times because I know Andrej is sad without me. Nobody loves him in that house. Nobody in the whole world loves him as much as I do. Mama doesn't understand me. Daddy doesn't understand me either. They say we could never marry. They say strange things. They think I'm a good girl because I'm so quiet. But I don't wanna be good. I'll never be good again. I'll get up tomorrow while it's still dark, so that no one could see me. Then I'll go visit Andrej. I'll tell him I love him. I'll bring him daffodils from the garden because snowdrops are off already. I think he won't laugh now. And he'll surely say, I love you my big brave little girl.

Translated by the author

POLONA GLAVAN

Actually

POLONA GLAVAN

"**S**ay something," she says as she pulls her arm from mine, and rests it on the pillow. "Talk."

"What about?" I ask, and raise my head.

"Anything," she answers. "Weather, politics, the two of us. Whatever you want. Just talk."

"Why?" I ask.

"Just for the heck of it," she says. "I'd like to hear you."

"Hear me?" I raise my eyebrows.

"Yes," she says. "For once I'd like to really, fully hear you. I have no clue what sort of person you are when you talk."

"But you do know what sort of person I am."

"How would I?" she asks. "How on earth could I know?"

"But we talk about one thing or another all the time."

"Possibly," she says and looks at me. "But I'd still like you to talk. I want you to talk to me, get it off your chest. . . . Whatever."

"Baby," I say.

"It doesn't matter if I listen or not," she says. "Maybe I'll be lost in my thoughts, or stare at the ceiling, or fall asleep. I just want you to talk. To me only."

"Yeah," I retort.

She falls silent for a moment and squeezes the fingers of my left hand.

"Talk about what will happen next," she says.

"When, next?" I ask.

"Next," she says. "Like tomorrow morning."

"I'll be in love with you," I say.

"Tomorrow morning?"

"Yes," I say. "I'll fall in love watching you sleep."

"Am I beautiful when I sleep?" she asks.

"You are," I say. "You look so innocent. I always fall in love when I watch you sleep."

"I don't believe you."

"What do you mean that you don't believe me?" I ask and raise myself on my elbow. "Can there be anything more truthful than someone falling in love with you while watching you sleep?"

"It's possible," she shrugs. "I haven't thought about it yet."

"Then think about it now," I say. "Think about that fairy tale where . . . Which one was it? Cinderella?"

"Sleeping Beauty," she says.

"That's right. I forgot."

"Shame on you. How can you forget such a beautiful fairy tale?"

"I remember it all right," I say. "Just the name escapes me."

"Really?" She lifts her left eyebrow suspiciously.

"Really." I nod. "Look, Sleeping Beauty pricks her finger and falls asleep for one hundred years. Then a prince comes, falls in love with her, and wakes her up with a kiss. Then they live happily ever after, and have a bunch of kids." I take a breath and look at the ceiling. "See, I remember everything. Just names—that's the problem."

"Will you wake me up with a kiss?" she asks.

"No," I shake my head. "I'll let you sleep."

"Why?"

"So I can watch you longer," I say. "Sleeping."

"What if I'm already awake?" she asks. "Will you still be in love with me?"

"I don't know," I say. "It depends."

"On what?"

"Well," I shrug. "On the look you give me. Let's say you were leaning on your elbow and looking at me mockingly, or, perhaps, tenderly for a change.... Well, if your look is mocking, I'll fall in love for sure."

"What if I'm gone?" she asks. "What then?"

"Then I'll cry," I say.

"What if I hear you crying and bring you a handkerchief?" she asks. "Trimmed with lace, with my monogram embroidered on it. What then?"

"Then I'll fall in love with you even more."

"But you know I'd do no such thing."

"Too bad," I say. "Because if you don't wipe away my tears, I'll hang myself."

"Don't you dare," she says. "Just try it, and I'll take you down from the rope, and smack you hard. Do you want that to happen? Do you?"

"Why don't you join me?" I tousle her hair above her eyes. "You can't even imagine how romantic it would be to be found with our necks in the same noose."

"Ooh," she says. And, even though it's dark in the room I see a glint of interest in her eyes. "You're right. That would be wickedly romantic. Should we do it?"

"We can," I say. "Or we can do something even better."

"Like what?"

"We can buy a heart-shaped porcelain bowl," I say. "Then we cut our veins and bleed to death into it together. What do you think?"

"And then our blood will cake, and people will pour it out and put it on our grave?" She added, her voice radiating with involvement. "Super! And in the shape of a heart. Totally crazy!"

"Yes," I say, and I pause in thought.

"You know what else would be awesome?" she finally continues after a while and leans over me.

"What?"

"If we went to a railroad crossing and lie on two separate tracks," she says. "We hold hands and wait for a train. When we are crushed to pieces, only our held hands will remain. This would be, like, totally legendary, can you imagine it?"

"You're right. Let's do it."

She again falls silent for a moment.

"What do you think will be the first thing that happens afterward?" she asks after a while.

"Everybody will talk about us."

"That," she says, "And maybe more."

"They may create a cult of us."

"Yes," she warms to the idea. "And everyone will follow us."

"It will give the authorities a major headache," I add.

"Parents will be sick with worry."

"And sociologists. And psychiatrists. And believers."

"The whole world will turn upside down," she nods. "And half of the universe."

"Can you imagine all of the newspapers writing about us?"

"And the photographs," she adds. "And background checks. And the collecting of evidence."

"Suddenly everyone will remember they knew us," I say. "That always happens in such cases."

"I think this can become a great theme for a tragedy," she suggests, in her professionally jaded style.

"And for paintings," I add.

"They'll make movies about us," she says.

"Yes."

"Teach about us in schools," she added.

"That, too."

"This will be our legacy," she says.

"We'll last through the ages," I complement her.

"Absolutely."

"The whole world will know about us."

"And the universe too."

"And eternity. Can you imagine—eternity!"

"Yes."

We fall silent.

"Yes," she says quietly after a while. "Life will be full of our death. Everywhere there'll be just us two. But, actually, we'll be nowhere."

"What do you mean, nowhere?"

"That's the fact," she says. "We won't exist."

"Why not?"

"Why, why, why," she says. "Because. Because nothing will ever change. You'll wake up, get dressed, have coffee with me, steal my last cigarette, and leave. You'll leave, just like you always do. And go to her."

"I won't," I feebly try to lie.

"Oh, come on," she says. "Stop fooling yourself. Why wouldn't you? Why would this particular Wednesday be the day you don't care to be with her? Can you tell me? I don't think you can."

"I can."

"Then why?" she asks.

"Because I'll fall in love with you."

Her smile glows briefly in the dark.

"Oh, baby," she strokes my cheek mercifully. "Be honest at least with yourself, if you can't tell the truth to me. You know, I figured it out a long time ago. Why do you say that to me, baby, why?"

"Because it's true," I protest. "You'll see."

She turns on her back and stares at the ceiling.

"I already see too much."

"See what?" I ask.

"Plenty," she says. "Too much. Everything. I'm aware of so many things that I know each and every detail. Everything is familiar and everything is the same. I see, for instance, that simply nothing is happening. Nothing is changing. Everything remains the same, just like it's always been. Everything."

"Death is not the same."

"Yes, it is. It's the same."

"It can't be," I object.

"And why not?" she asks. "What is changing about it? Is it prettier than it used to be? Uglier? Kind or unkind? I think none of the above."

"It can't be the same."

"But it is," she says. "Except that we talk about it now. Okay, *that's* different. But only that. The rest is just the same as yesterday, today, last year, every day. Don't say it's not true."

I say nothing. She too falls silent.

"You know what," she says after a while. "I ..."

"What?"

She stares at me for a few moments. Then she opens her mouth eagerly to say something, but changes her mind, and closes her eyelids.

"Nothing," she says and buries her nose behind my ear.

"Tell me," I move away and look into her eyes.

"It's nothing," she withdraws her gaze.

"Tell me," I insist. "Please."

"It's nothing. I mean, nothing important. Just a small, silly idea. Totally trivial. In fact, I can't remember what I was going to say. Forget it."

"Are you sure?"

"Yes," she says. "Trust me."

She leans over me and kisses me on the mouth.

"Sweet dreams," she says, and withdraws her lips just as I snatch at them. "Sleep well, love."

"You, too."

She buries her nose under my collarbone and closes her eyes. I stay awake for a while longer, staring at the ceiling. When I hear her peaceful even breathing, I decide to join her. I wrap my arm around her waist, and we remain this way until morning. Long black shadows blend with a still silence. Actually, we really don't know how to have a conversation.

Translated by SONJA KRAVANJA

POLONA GLAVAN

To See Žiri and Die

TOMAŽ KOSMAČ

I have never been to Žiri.
Really never, though it is only about 10 miles away from Idrija, where
I've been wearing out most of my present life. It used to be even nearer
when I was a child and later a callow youth, deeply naïve and innocent.
The cottage where I used to live with my parents was right on the road
to Žiri. Every day cars with workers rolled along it, merrily raising dust,
so that I used to have to dampen the bumpy gravel road. The way of
preventing constant dustiness changed with progress. At first we had to
splash the road with stale oil and burnt cooking oil. Eventually, the main
road was paved, and the villagers' innovative ways of stopping and less-
ening the dusty clouds were effectively ended.

Along with modernization, buses were introduced, and the people
clung to the regular schedule in the morning, at 2 p.m., and in the evening,
operating in coordination with the workers' shifts. In this way the line
could make a little profit, since the traveling cars were only partly occupied. I often wished to get on one of them and finally take a look at the
famous Žiri. And as is often the case with people who think a lot about
something, I was no exception—I never hit the road. There were rumors
that cheap shoes could be bought at the Alpina shop in Žiri. I was convinced of this, for a great number of mountain lovers walked around in
ski shoes. Our family bought a pair of them as well. I myself would
never go out in sports footwear.

There was another sort of rumor going around: that the people of
Žiri disliked the people of Idrija, and that they liked beating them black
and blue. I was not afraid of that. I get drunk easily, become sociable,

make contacts, but there is not a trace of violence in my blood. I could never quite believe those rumors, which must have been triggered by bullies. For instance, the rumor that I was there, and that they were having a fight but they did not touch me. Reading between the lines: they tried to avoid any contact with me, as I was such a macho! They are the kind of freaks who brag about being always stopped by the cops because the cops pick on them. The point they try to make is that cops cannot get them because they are such fiendish shysters who, when inspected, always have a vehicle in full working order that, however, had had a destructive defect the day before. Fortunately, they have a sixth sense warning them about any danger, and in this way they never pay the fine because they have a knack for somehow eliminating the defect just in time. And they will still be standing proudly by the road, raising their vain heads and smiling meaningfully to each passerby so that they would be noticed: "They have stopped me, just look at them, they have stopped *me* again!" In this and other similar ways they try to deceive people, they try to hide their empty unexcited lives, rolling on slowly and monotonously like a long and quiet river with no waves or bends. Deep in my subconscious I used to imagine that as a child I had once gone through the settlement of Žiri. And indeed I found it unbelievable that I had never been brought to this neighboring town, which stretched out at an arm's length from me, and I slowly started to believe that I must have been there once. This could be one of the explanations of a state of déjà vu. A certain hitherto unknown place, impression, or experience is recognized as something you have already seen or experienced. However, it must have been only an image inside your head telling you that you must have experienced it!

Once I was on a drinking spree for quite a time, not because of the holidays, but just like that, for no purpose really. Life varies, it has its ups and downs, just like the moon waxing and waning. I had plunged into a crisis, I was lost, without any ideas, in black menopause. It went so far that, lonely as I was, I took to drinking at the bus station. Sometimes I do get overwhelmed by a nonsensical feeling for no reason. Leaning against the bar, I was toasting myself. The bus station was the last resort, the lowest dump of all. A suburb of hell visited by ultra-lost souls and by those few pensioners who wait in their frailty for the last mercy bullet.

An invitation from Rupert, an all-but-forgotten friend, aroused me from my lethargy. The hands of the clock were showing six in the evening when he announced he was going to celebrate New Year's Eve in the Pol-jane Valley.

"Come along," he said. "I'm going to my girlfriend's. She isn't what you call a beauty, but she's the best I've ever had."

I knew most of his girlfriends. They were not bad. I thought it a good idea to join him, as I had nothing better to do. The thought of going on a trip was a gift from heaven. A God-given hint that it was time for me to make an effort and stop this lethargy. Fifteen minutes later we were sitting on the bus.

"Where are we going?"

"To Logatec."

"Why Logatec? You said you were heading for Žiri."

"You get to Žiri through Logatec."

"I didn't know that. Why aren't we going through Razpotje? Why are we taking the longer way 'round?" I was teasing him because I was annoyed.

"At this hour you can only get there this way. Particularly today."

"Fuck New Year's Eve!"

But in the end I decided not to worry too much. Actually, I was depressed because I had not drunk anything for half an hour, and I was pleased at the same time to have finally made a move and gotten out of Idrija. I should have shaken off that cesspool before. I had enough cash, and if you have the will you can do a lot of things with cash. It makes you feel secure, ransoms your worries, helps you crush and bury them. However, for the past few days, I seemed to have no wish to do that. We got out at the Logatec bus station, went to the pub's trough to kill time over some drinks and animated conversation until the next departure, and then rolled onto the Žiri bus. It was lonely inside; there were not many passengers. Besides us two there was an extremely attractive and nice young blonde who, with her tits, had settled in one of the front seats. The beauty of her face was a bit spoiled by excessive makeup, and above all by the little red shoes at the end of her long legs. I was hoping that they were not the latest model from the Alpina.

The bus conductor walked flabbily down the aisle dragging his long face toward the back of the bus.

"Where to?"

"To the end of the line."

A plastic bag on the seat between us caught his half-open eye.

"Have you got a drink? You could offer me one."

"We haven't got a bottle opener."

I pointed at the cap on the wine bottle whose metal stood in the way of our benevolence.

The fare collector reached for the bottle; he skillfully removed the obstacle with his teeth and took a deep draught. We followed his example. He hung about and we spent a few minutes emptying the contents together. When he had quenched his thirst, he said, "The ride's on me," and he quietly went back to the driver.

"What a cool guy. There should be more of his kind in the world."

"It has happened before," said Rupert.

I did not believe him, but it was a phenomenal feeling. That singular generous and uncommon gesture was able to bring about what I had been seeking for a long time but could not find. It dragged me out of my apathy. I felt life coming back into my body. The bus was rushing down the narrow gravel road, leaning dangerously over on the endless bends. Because of the friendly drinking, the ride seemed well suited to my fiery state. Rupert casually expressed his worries. But it was more for the sake of conversation than out of real uneasiness.

"Those two are loaded. I hope they don't overturn us somewhere."

TOMAŽ KOSMAČ

"Don't worry, they're in control. They must drive around these parts every day."

The baton was being passed from hand to hand, our fears disappeared, and we were melting in a festive atmosphere of relaxation. In the middle of darkness, split by colorful light bulbs hanging in the balcony of a nearby house, the humming engine stopped. The conductor addressed his sparse audience, his legs astride, announcing, "You are all invited to the pub for a drink!"

"Haven't we had enough? We have to finish the ride," the driver meekly mumbled.

"There's no hurry. I do everything by the book all year 'round. We can afford to give ourselves a treat for once. On New Year's Eve, at least, if at no other time."

He and his companion left the bus. None of us three joined them. Rupert and I, we still had a drop of wine in the bottle, and we really did not want to get comatose too early. Also, cash was no problem, and we did not want to go on needlessly fleecing our generous fare collector. The painted beauty made no sound. She sank into her seat and stared into the promising future expressionless.

After the refreshment stop we continued on our way. The headlights on the square metal front of the bus were throwing light onto the snake-like landscape. Now long, then short, and at times no lights at all. The lights, blinking on and off, were giving the driver some problems, and he was losing control of the regular lighting system. When he finally switched off all the lights and other electrical devices, we all, being used to frequent electricity reductions, reached the destination safely. Rupert, who was acquainted with the grim-looking back roads, headed toward his mistress's home. Suddenly he stopped.

"I haven't got a present. Let's go first to the pub and drop by at her place later. She doesn't know I'm here, and she isn't expecting a visit. I'd rather surprise her with my hands full."

"Or with your head full," I said.

We walked down the high street of the El Dorado. A festive atmosphere could be felt everywhere. The settlement was decorated, cries of joy could be heard, colorful lights were inviting us into their embrace. We peeked into two or three red-curtained dives, but they were all more than full. In the end we knocked at the door of a senior citizens' club. Without vanity or discontent they generously let us join them. We looked pleasant and were youthfully dressed. We were two inquisitive young men who needed a drop of magical luck.

There was an accordion playing in the room. The entrance into the music room was immediately to the right of a promising door opening into paradise. The elderly people were happy and noisy, all of them in a generous, boisterous mood. The tables were all occupied. We had brought them a small piece of wormwood. A middle-aged man with a fur cap on his head and with thick glasses on his nose invited us to his table in a nearby corner. His companion was a woman with visible signs of brain deficiency. Rupert merrily greeted them, and we sat down on the vacant seats. Probably the only ones in the spacious room. A bottle of white wine appeared on the table.

"This is Cosmo, a student of surgery," he introduced me.

"I work at the morgue in Ljubljana." I was ready to play the game. "I make sections of corpses."

"I thought I had seen you before," said Fur-Cap.

"I don't think so. I deal with dead people."

"Really? I work as an assistant at transporting bodies. I come to Ljubljana frequently."

"I still don't remember you. I work at night and rarely come outside."

"That must be it. We bring the dead to the entrance only. Then they are taken over by others," he would not give up.

"I work there only occasionally. We practice postmortems on the dead and try to improve our knowledge. We take shifts, and on average

I get mine once every two weeks. Otherwise I practice on the wounded and the injured at the medical center."

"Then you must be a doctor!"

"I will be one," I explained modestly.

Fur-Cap offered me his hand and, despite my frequent protests that it was unnecessary, called me sir all evening. He said he remembered me by the glasses I was wearing. I told him I had had the round-rimmed ones for only a month and that before I had a classical model. Like the ones he had. He was flattered and became even more convinced of the fact that he had already had the honor of meeting me. I just could not persuade him that he was wrong. Doctors are always overrated.

In the meantime Rupert made close contact with the man's retarded companion. They were holding hands. On the table, in full view of everyone. I jabbed at his knee to make him aware that he had gone too far in showing his attentions. I did not like his taking advantage of hospitality in such a dirty way. He grinned and suddenly disappeared somewhere with the unattractive young girl.

"Don't mind him," I said to Fur-Cap. "Rupert can't help taking a bite at every woman's body."

"It's all right, sir," he hastily replied. "I tell you, I only know her casually."

"Don't call me sir, I'm nobody special. Only one of many surgeons."

"It's improper to call you by your name. Care for another drink, sir?"

I took the money from my pocket, but he refused the offered equality and ordered another bottle at his expense. We again started to discuss the butcher's work. Rupert returned and was followed by the contented girl. Without any superfluous reproaches, we emptied the flask in harmonious accord. Midnight was inevitably approaching. We had to say good-bye. While walking in the fresh cold air I turned to Rupert.

"You didn't screw her, did you?"

"Of course, I did!"

"You're irrepressible."

"She may be wacky, but she sure knows how to fuck!"

I could not approve of his words nor of his deeds, I did not mock, and I did not contradict. Everyone is free to do what he wants if they don't hurt anyone else. I wisely kept silent and took a sip from the bottle we had bought for his true love.

"Don't drink that!"

"It's better if it's not full. So we can say the liqueur is homemade. Made especially for her."

"You're right," he said and took a bunch of liquid himself.

We took turns scratching the label off the bottle and refreshing ourselves with the yellowish liquid as we neared the apartment. At the height of our bliss, we pressed the soft bell. The door was opened by a dark, stocky girl, with big breasts, strong legs, a good face, and not at her happiest to have guests. Beside her there was her ten- or twelve-year-old brother.

"Rupert, what are you doing here?"

"I came to wish you a happy New Year. This is my friend, a student of surgery."

"Cut it out," I said shifting awkwardly from foot to foot.

"Well, come in, now you're here. But you will have to leave soon because my parents are coming home at one o'clock."

In the living room we poured each other the homemade liqueur, which he had vehemently handed to her with an obligatory kiss on the cheek. In the soft chair opposite us there was the painted model from the bus. She still had those little red shoes on. She was terribly attractive and at the same time repulsive because of her cold attitude. Our dialogue consisted of exchanging clichés. I was getting nervous and wanted to leave as soon as possible, as I did not in any way belong to the mosaic of present company. I was fidgeting nervously on the couch and concentrated on the brat who was complacently showing me his album of stickers. There were some pictures missing. With great interest

I was, superfluously, looking at the empty spaces in the album. I promised the boy the missing pictures. At the same time I kept looking at the model, who was calm, unaffected, stoic, and was pretending to be absorbed in watching a TV program. I hated her and loved her because she ignored me so intelligently, because I had to pretend to be sober, though I was drunk, because I liked her and I did not like her, because I wanted to make contact with her and because I wanted to get far away. The girl surpassed me in every respect. I fell in love with her and was afraid to end up a fool if I tried to be witty, a treasury of bad jokes and excessively enthusiastic. Exactly like the program she was watching. Little Red Shoes, I, and the album, we were all helplessly exchanging glances, and in our embarrassment we cast our eyes at the flop of a party. Rupert and the dark girl exchanged no words of love, they were not engaged in any dreamy embraces, and there was no sign of any glances of commitment. Their love was cooling down and nearing its end. What was left was just the one terrible nightmare of leaving as soon as possible. Finally Rupert and I decided to say good-bye. The dark girl's parents were supposedly on their way home. Now it was time for the dark girl's long-expected joy, the joy of relief. We parted smilingly and with our mouths full of promises to meet again. We all wanted to part from one another as soon as possible.

Outside we found ourselves victimized on the plains of hopelessness. There was nowhere we could warm our cold balls. The small town was quiet and was mourning in the dark. The pubs did not welcome any prodigals, the bus lines were not operating. We crept to a nearby haystack and tried to spend the night on a tractor parked among the farmer's tools. We kept our asses together on the cold seat. Rupert unzipped his winter coat and produced the half-empty bottle of liqueur. The dark girl had slipped it to him as a farewell present. He unscrewed the top, and we warmed ourselves until the last drop was gone.

"What now? We can't spend the night here. If there had only been some hay," I sighed.

"Let's go home."

"How?"

"On foot."

The die was cast, and we made it to the main road. Like every main road this one offered two possibilities. I claimed we had to turn left, and Rupert insisted on turning right. In the end we each went in our own supposedly right direction.

I was trying to find my way between the houses for a long time, dragging endlessly and doubting my choice to go left. I did not want to go back or go in another direction. It was important to persist, though it seemed more and more strange that the way back kept dragging across the plains for so long when I should have started to go up already. When I left the pale houses behind me, my optimism started to grow. I was self-assured and knew that the solution could not be far away. I was walking relaxed for a long, long time, and by each of the haystacks, which were always standing like soldiers close by, I stopped to find a little necessary warmth for my forced overnight sleep. Each hope turned out to be an illusion. The miles that I had walked multiplied, and then a light shone behind my back, announcing an approaching car. I tried to balance my body with dignity and lifted my thumb, trying not to sway too much, to get an uncompromising lift. The vehicle stopped but the sight of it was not very tempting. Through the open window, a policeman's head appeared asking me for my ID. With my numb fingers I took my ID from my pocket and handed it to him for inspection. The policeman wanted some information.

"It says it all," I gently uttered.

"Don't fuck with me. Your name and surname!"

I made him happy by complying with his request.

"Go on."

"What do you mean?"

"Where do you live, when were you born, what do you do?"

"In security."

"What *in security?*"

"I work."

"And you're from Idrija?"

"Yes."

"Where are you going?"

"Home."

His companion, meanwhile, had my truthfulness and other trifles checked out on the radio.

"Well, okay, you can go. You're nearly there," he gave me back my ID.

"Would you give me a lift?"

"Where to?"

"To Idrija."

The window was pulled up and harshly ended any thought of an official service. The Zastava turned around, made a circle, and returned toward Žiri, where it just had come from. I started to walk faster and continued from where I had been interrupted, naïvely hoping for better times. I started to sober up and, consequently, my mood changed for the worse. When the next haystack appeared in front of me, I did not give it much thought. I headed for it, made a pile of some hay that lay scattered on the ground, found a few boards, and covered myself.

I got up, freezing, in the first morning hours when the light started to remove its night veils. I couldn't feel my soles. I felt pins and needles in my frostbitten feet. I walked feeling nothing and moved along like a robot. There was another haystack along the road. The road was winding into aimlessness. I sat down into the snow that lay around in patches and waited resignedly. I squeezed my blue fingers helplessly between my painful knees, my teeth chattered, and in the deadly silence I tried to catch some possible sound of salvation. It came in the approaching form of a humming car engine and was followed a bit later by the visible shape of a Fiat. I pulled myself up from the ground and lifted my hand. Luck was on my side. I opened the heavenly gate.

"I'm going to Idrija."

"You've got to turn around. I'm going to Škofja. Idrija is in the other direction."

I gave thanks for the information, closed the car door, and walked back toward my starting point. I gave up hitchhiking. I was too exhausted. I started to walk again, and in my tiredness I cursed the policemen on night duty. They had fucked me up. I wanted to lie somewhere to the side and close my eyes forever. If only my frozen bones would stop hurting and this feeling of helpless weakness would leave me. My toes started to wake up, and each step hurt like hell. I began meeting silent houses again, lonely haystacks, and more and more objects leading me into the familiar settlement. I was absolutely exhausted when I reached the bus station. On the front panel of the bus, which had its engine already started, I read "Žiri-Logatec." I intended to get on it and crossed the road. The driver closed the bus doors and drove away. I chased the stinking fumes. All I caught were gas vapors; a soft and warm seat was quickly disappearing in the distance. It occurred to me that Žiri was like hell—once you enter, there's no escape. The angel's chariot disappeared beyond the horizon, renouncing my soul, which had become stuck in the winter landscape, lonely and with no hope of deliverance.

I returned to the station, and after reading the timetable, found out that the next help for travelers would not be coming for four hours. I took a seat in the pub and let myself be served a rum. When I ran out of money, the bus came. Drunk and resigned, I shrugged my shoulders and slowly swayed on homeward. This time in the right direction. I was soon picked up by a vehicle, and after each mile a new idyllic image of life appeared. Žiri, my suffering, and my critical agony that had lasted for weeks started slowly but surely to lose the ground beneath their feet. Energy again started to pour into me.

Translated by IRENA ZORKO

TOMAŽ KOSMAČ

Out of Order

ALEŠ ČAR

this is a story about love. And about happiness. In the end, it is a kind of happiness if a person simply knows that there is something in the air before one word is spoken. That's how it was that night. Ten minutes of silence and a giraffe on the television screen can actually say an awful lot.

"What's happening?"

"Nothing."

A minute passed during which I figured out that she'd had more to drink than usual for this time of day.

"Well?"

"Well nothing." Another minute. "I don't know what's with me." After a few more minutes. "I don't know ... as if I were psychologically obsessed," she was silent. "As if a part of me was psychologically obsessed with you."

The cabbage roll stuck in my throat. I looked at her.

"No shit, please." I looked at her, she was seriously plastered.

"I don't play that game."

I threw the rest of the cabbage roll into the garbage and walked into the bathroom. Half a Valium. I heard her walking across to the refrigerator, must be to get another whiskey, and then going into the bathroom. I knew she was on the verge of tears, I knew I was helpless and that made me panic a little; above all it made me mad, for I can smell tears a mile away. The sourness of the skin, the hair, the odor from the mouth. They all spoke volumes. I thought about the last few days, weeks—nothing special had happened. I looked at myself in the mirror above the sink and saw myself standing in front of the medicine cabinet, all five boxes of sedatives in my hand and feverishly wondering where I could hide them before she flushed the toilet. The next second she was in the bathroom and I was still standing there numb. I looked into the pupils of her eyes: there were not just three shots of cheap whiskey in there, there were pills too. And she really was near to tears.

I shook the boxes. "How many did you take?"

"Five."

Five is not a dose that is life threatening, but it is a dose that is fascinating. Taking the sedatives with me, I sat down in the study. In the ten minutes that followed, she was transformed into a swaying sculpture, dripping with drunkenly laconic remarks. After two rounds, she stopped by the bathroom door and, in between her sobs, demanded that I immediately make it clear if I intended to throw her out of the apartment. I answered that the door was always open, and that I wasn't thinking about that right then. I knew that she would leave it open. Every time I'm reminded of a squid. Ink in the enemy's eyes. I knew and could hear she was crying. And she was waiting for me to look at her. For it to start. Our dance.

I stared at a table. Actually at a book that was lying on the table. Actually at one spot on the book. One letter. The letter of defeat. Just like every time before this, and now again, also. Because I didn't have any choice: I would look at her sooner or later. I always did. I lifted my gaze. What else?

As it happens I have a problem. Tanya cries often and copiously. She herself says her willpower cannot cope with everything. She feels the tears in her throat unbidden, she says, and once there, they simply flow. A fact that is more physiologically than emotionally conditioned. Well, this is where the story really begins: every time she cries, I get an erection. I don't have anything to do with it; to use Tanya's words, it is a more

ALEŠ ČAR

physiologically than emotionally conditioned reaction to her tears. Actually, the situation is much worse than that: it's enough if we're just in the trenches, if the air is tense with argument and shouting, if we are lying to each other, denouncing or humiliating each other. Frequently, that's enough, he announces himself down there, and in his Victorian atmosphere begins to meditate on, yes, her cunt.

I screamed. I couldn't do anything else.

"Why are you doing this to me? Why are you fucking humiliating me?!"

A second later, I was alone in the study. Then I found her in the armchair, white as the wall, tears and mascara running into her mouth. Horrible. She was looking right between my legs and smiling, or so it seemed to me. She allowed me to lift her up, to lay her on the couch and cover her and make her a strong cup of coffee. I stirred in two big spoonfuls of salt instead of sugar and, after the first sip, helped her to the toilet bowl where everything she had in her stomach came flying out.

Hippopotami had meanwhile replaced the giraffes on the television, and after fifteen minutes she managed to smile weakly.

She apologized, we searched for air.

"Fuck it. You owe me," I said.

"I love you."

A few minutes later, a bloody sanitary napkin was flying through the room and, together with a pair of panties, landed on the handle of the closet door. Later, when we were peacefully smoking, pressed between the sheets, she showed me the puncture marks from paper clips on her hands and the bruises on her forehead. All that was supposedly from the arguments of that same day. I looked at Tanya's shadow in the dusk and strangely crooked thoughts flashed through my mind. Once again, to be sure. I said nothing. Charles Lloyd on saxophone was the evening's guest, a scene of spider webs in the darkness, a sense of being wrung out, sweetly sleepy.

As I said, this is a story about love. In spite of all the odd physiological or indeed emotional reactions, in the final analysis it's all the same. Tanya and I won't let it go. At this specific moment in the development of our relationship, there was simply no option but to open a common front against Him, the third in the apartment. We treated him as a person with his own will, as some kind of capricious, annoying kid, who, for the sake of peace and quiet in the apartment, had to be constantly attended to and have his various wishes fulfilled. And finally those situations when we were united against him were actually moments of happiness. A split was rather more difficult—a fight on two fronts simultaneously, as above, against Him and against Tanya at the same time. And yet I persevered. As a slave to Tanya and a slave to my Prick.

And so in the evening after the fight, I walked through empty Ljubljana and looked at the shreds of fog above the river. Here and there something shuffled in the dusk and a duck flew up out of the mist. A faint drizzle in some manner thickened the air into a real springtime decay. I considered that I might say something more about Tanya's past, that I might say something more about myself, about our first meeting years ago, that I might talk about the reasons for our marriage, perhaps something about Tanya's fear of giving birth or about my fear of heights. I might; but it was just the usual story of two people: a meeting, a successful compromise that sooner or later means a shared life, meaning that everything is more inert, which in the end means that we actually love each other or something like that. And that's all.

Unpleasantly wet from the drizzle, I went into the Zamorec Bar, where I was supposed to meet Tanya. She was already there, alone at the table in the corner, a whiskey in front of her. Besides her, there were about ten people in the little establishment, sitting around five tables and at the bar. Three were standing and talking with the waiter, two couples sat each at their own table, a middle-aged woman sat alone at a table and Tanya at another. I went to the bar. Whiskey. What kind? Any kind. I parked myself in the space diagonally across from Tanya. I observed the people, evaluated the situation, waited.

The middle-aged woman drinking at the neighboring table asked me for a light. I lit her cigarette and added a word or two but the conversation didn't take.

The couple on the other side of Tanya stood up, paid, and disappeared. I ordered another whiskey; two kids walked in and sat at the table that had been vacated next to Tanya. The woman next to me was talking about the film festival where she does public relations. I looked at her more carefully: a lady in her mid-forties, probably a little bit drunk, otherwise well dressed, a black pullover and a long black skirt with a long slit up the side. She wore a black scarf around her neck, short straight hair, dyed red. She works all day and treats herself to a whiskey before going home. . . . Yeah, she lives alone. Three years now. Divorced, of course. I looked beyond her: the two kids had connected with Tanya, involved her in their conversation. Tanya was openly flirting. I had to ask the woman to repeat her question.

"What do you do in life?"

I told her I was a midfield player with the Korotan Club. Where? National league, football. At first it didn't make any impression on the woman, and then, when she decided I was lying, she seemed pleased. We ordered another round; she paid.

Tanya disappeared into the bathroom. The boys didn't remove their eyes from her miniskirt all the way to the door. I tried to think of something to do, but couldn't decide. My middle-aged woman was talking about her weekend house in Bovec, how she invested everything in it, how she loved walking in the Alps, but last summer the earthquake took it away. Tanya returned from the bathroom and sat down at the table with the two boys. We caught each other's eyes right at the moment when the guy on Tanya's right went into action: first he leaned his leg against her thigh—she didn't react, just stared straight into my eyes—then he continued by pulling his leg back and pressing his knee between Tanya's legs. It had started. I stared at the top of the guy's head as he rubbed his knee against the inside of her thigh: tall, thin, in a leather jacket, short blond hair, a military backpack hanging on the chair behind him. . . . My mind made a quick cut.

A good six months ago, while I was looking at some shots, I caught sight of Tanya, while with one guy, flicking her red miniskirt in front of some other guy. I told the editor to freeze the picture: I saw Tanya's micro-miniskirt projected on all eight screens.

"Go frame by frame."

The hand in the clip slowly pulled away from the projected ass and in an abbreviated half-circle rose up to her hair, then it began to move back down to her waist and so on and so forth, and only after about ten seconds, I realized that all this bending and leaning meant her laughter.

"Stop."

The guy who was standing next to her in the clip was thin, tall, in wide military pants and a leather jacket, with spiky short blond hair and a military backpack across his shoulder. I remembered exactly. His face couldn't be made out. Only a trampled circle. She was definitely flirting. I spent the next half-hour flipping through prints, looking for the precise moment when she came into the concert hall during the applause after the second number, then for the moment when the guy came in. Other than Tanya he was the only one who came in seriously late. He missed a half a number more than Tanya did. At that moment, camera one was shooting close-ups of fingers on the solo saxophone (nothing could be seen of them here), and camera two showed a wide-angle shot of the whole band. The doors could be seen at the very edge of the shot. It slowly opened out further and I spotted the green pants and then the black leather jacket. I still couldn't see the face.

Cut.

The woman I was with looked at me confused, waiting for I don't know what. I finished my whiskey, apologized, got up decisively and went to the bathroom. I was leaning above the urinal trying to piss when the door opened for a second. Tanya looked in and made a beckoning movement. Then disappeared. I walked into the women's room. Two stalls. One locked.

"It's me."

Nothing.

A stream hit the porcelain then fell into the water.

"Tanya?"

Nothing.

Later, as I was waiting in the hallway, the woman appeared. At the same moment, Tanya emerged from the bathroom and, without looking at me, strode back to the bar. The woman asked me if I knew her since I'd been looking at her all night. Briefly and decisively, I denied it. Then the woman looked at me, openly flirting. I opened the door to the woman's bathroom for her. She slowly walked in, turned around and looked me straight in the eye. There was no doubt. I walked in after her, pulled a scrap of paper out of my inside pocket with, in big red letters, OUT OF ORDER, and stuck it on to the door of the stall. The words seemed appropriate, and with a laugh we closed the door behind us. We started the dance without wasting words. I lifted her skirt. Her stockings ended at the thigh, her narrow panties presented no obstacle. She leaned her head away from me so I couldn't kiss her, which suited me fine. As I energetically rubbed her, a sigh rose up from her bones and her belly, and right then the door to the bathroom opened. We stood still, held our breath and, *fuck it*, trembled. The steps went straight into the stall next to ours and shut themselves inside. I heard the sound of knocking against the bowl: three times, pause, and then two times. Tanya. I pushed the head of the woman hard down, and as she slowly began to suck, Tanya's eyes appeared above the top edge of the partition. One of the many times that we absently stared into each other's eyes across one barrier or another: reproachful, powerless, and encouraging all at the same time. Potent in our impotence. Certain in our uncertainty about whether to go ahead, together. Because of the two of us, clearly. And always the fresh extremity of uncertainty in those moments that we solved with the formula that everything that surrounded the pair of us was right here, and only because of us, pulling us apart came from us, from within the two of us. And if we needed three to stay together as two, then we would take a third. If we needed four, or five, six or more to stay together as two, then we would take them too.

Tanya's head disappeared, I heard a man's voice. It said some name or other three times in a row. I pulled out of the woman's mouth, still in a far from useful state, stepped on to the toilet seat and peeked over the door: standing outside was the guy with the leather jacket and the military trousers, and I no longer had any doubt that tonight wasn't the first time Tanya had met him.

I lowered myself down again. The guy must have noticed two pairs of feet under the door of our stall. Water could be heard falling into the toilet bowl, so loud that it drowned out their conversation. The woman wanted to continue with her efforts to animate me down below, but I stopped her and, with the tips of my fingers, firmly closed her eyelids. She grew calm, though I could see on her face that she was confused. I leaned in toward her face, let out a stream of spit, aiming at the ring of mascara around her eye: the spittle stretched out, fell slowly, so I adjusted and it hit her left eyelid. She opened her right eye, looked at me in surprise, but I firmly pressed the lid down again. The second time I missed and the saliva fell on the edge of her lips. The third time, I hit right below the right eye and smeared her lashes so it looked liked she'd been crying and, in that instant, I was ready: I turned her around, leaned her over the toilet, so that she was braced with her hands against the tiles above the seat, and plunged into her. We tried to control our breathing, the woman even untied the scarf around her neck and bit on it, though it probably wasn't necessary, for on the other side of the thin partition they had started to screw without compromise. We adjusted our rhythms to each other and ended pretty much at the same time.

ALEŠ ČAR

For a moment the four of us observed our reflections in the large mirror above the sink: red, sweaty, fogged-up gazes, a little confused.

Holding each other tightly, Tanya and I headed out along the empty street. Though neither of us had an umbrella, and the rain was falling more and more heavily now, we didn't take a taxi. For an instant, we were alone in the city, *fuck it,* alone in the world. And perhaps truly happy. We walked through the streets, the rain beginning to smear the mascara around Tanya's eyes, and we held each other tighter and tighter, crept more and more into each other, pushed our tongues deeper and deeper into each other, somehow connected with one another. Obsessed? As if psychologically obsessed? Shit, whatever it was, we were passing into next circle of exhaustion, as it is called, into the next circle of love.

Translated by ERICA JOHNSON DEBELJAK

Everything Is Going to Be All Right

ANDREJ MOROVIČ

*i*t was in a city that seemed like every other northern American city. We made an exception and decided to take a standard sightseeing tour by bus.

We were stopped near yet another monument. Our little group had hardly moved at all when I noticed a black man in one of the numerous puddles. He was lying in it in an amazingly natural manner. It stopped me dead. Tall, strong, and handsome. Next to him or, rather, under him was a woman wriggling, as the female tourist from Germany would say. They were having sexual intercourse. Together. It really turned me on. The puddle was right next to the sidewalk, not exactly a large one but deep enough. And all the time cars were driving past splashing the water around. The woman went away, and I wanted at any cost to get into the puddle. Which I managed to do. I knew that you were probably already absorbed in admiring the characteristics of some architectural master-piece, and I did not have to worry much. I did not care for anything else. I tossed my head backward and closed my eyes. As if I had been injected into a hologram, I suddenly pictured my own little primrose to myself, abnormally blown up and beautifully spread out, so that its deep pink inside could be seen. The black man's hand was scooping the brownish liquid and splashing his palm into it, as if we had been playing some kind of infantile game. I did not like it and I said to him, "Come on, cut it out." We did not want to hang around in that puddle anymore. And we went into another one that was half-hidden under our bus. I was not particularly impressed by its depth. The black man sat down in it. I quickly made sure the bus was empty and threw myself, without an overture, on his bombastically swollen organ. I licked, sucked, and took it in with an insatiable pleasure. Well, I gave him a fantastic oral fuck. And then I looked up again, and there were a lot of shocked faces looking. Fat fathers and mothers and children with baseball caps—all of them pressing their noses against the bus windows, staring fixedly at us. I quickly got up and got on the bus. I was immensely ashamed but, fortunately, you did not notice anything, and that was the most important thing. The driver released the clutch so abruptly that he almost broke the gear shift. The rest of the ride I was on tenterhooks, trembling that you would start listening to the malevolent whispers coming to your ears from all the sides, and that you would put two and two together. But you were deep in your thoughts, and you were so handsome. When the time came, you got off. I don't know why, but I didn't get off with you. I was paralyzed or something, and the bus kept on driving and driving. I had to wait for it to make another round, and that was a goddamned long time. Of course, you were no longer at the bus stop. I looked around for you in vain. I was sure it was the right place, but the neighborhood seemed strange and unfamiliar all the same. I found myself in the middle of some square or other running down toward a lake glittering like leaden silver. It was surrounded by skyscrapers that made me feel anxious. They only had front windows so that the people living there were forced to look at a deformed replica of the Statue of Liberty, which stood in the middle of the water, looking threatening and evil. Suddenly I recognized a small detail that assured me I had not got lost after all. Soon after that I found you.

A man with a serious expression on his face approached us and introduced himself as our guide. We started a conversation that fit the surroundings well. Despite the uneasy, almost terrifying atmosphere, we knew this would be our home because *all* the outcasts lived here. We followed our coordinator with mixed feelings, almost mechanically. On the one hand, we felt as if we were being taken to the slammer, and on the other hand we were happy that we would not have to live anymore with

ANDREJ MOROVIČ

any other members of society. We stopped in front of the door of an apartment. To our surprise, our names were already engraved on the plate below the peephole. We entered, went straight to the window and opened it. We were at a dizzying height. We could see the ground far below us. The glassy surface of the motionless lake was bathed in the pure gold of sunshine. A unique view. One that in an instant heightens the feelings. When you gently put your arms around my hips, it almost hurt. And when I put my head on your shoulder, the nerves in my ears moaned with pleasure.

Ah, it was an unearthly peace, announcing some future when everything, I mean really everything, would be over. I gazed at the green oxidized face of the Statue of Liberty; I bored into it. I wondered how it had got all that evil amid this otherwise harmonious utopia. And then, incredibly, the statue secretly, but unquestionably, winked at me.

And there was no more doubt: everything was going to be all right.

Translated by IRENA ZORKO

In the Evenings We Go Out Together

ANDREJ MOROVIČ

*A*nd we always go somewhere else.

This time we visit a street in the Mitte district where an increasing number of alternative bars are scattered all around. To our great surprise we discover that working women, or their accountants, have chosen the same site for their market stall. It is here that the flower of Berlin prostitution nowadays does its solicitation. The ladies are professionally and quite offensively dressed, and they tolerate the stares of those driving past them with a pride and an indifference bordering on contempt. Compared to them, the freedom fighters from the traditional promenade in the west part of the city fade away.

We stop and watch them work. There is heavy traffic, lots of cars slow down but drive on empty as if their drivers were only testing the market.

A little to one side, yet in full view of everyone, stands a golden Mercedes with its engine running. In it there is a large man with curly hair and rugged features that cannot be completely hidden behind the dark windows.

When it starts drizzling, he suddenly but smoothly pulls out. He stops for a moment in front of the first employee in the line; the trunk is automatically raised, he waits for the lady to take out a pink umbrella and moves on to the next one.

A fascinatingly polished operation. Like changing tires in Formula One pits.

We discuss the profession itself and the relation between whore and pimp.

My message could be condensed as poor women or slaves to brutal masters, to heroin or to similar addictions. Her discussion is more inclined toward "La belle de jour"—the huge need to fuck, and the pimp probably being only necessary as an orientation point, as a kind of a friend and as an exemplar of fucking.

In the end we would really like to see at least one of the women enter a car and drive into the night; we would like some kind of a souvenir. No such luck.

We go from one bar to another looking for people who are willing and able to peek just an inch out of their shells for the fun of it, people who might plunge themselves into an open-ended play.

Nothing but sadness.

We try our luck at an astro party. Aluminum and silver glitter everywhere. Blond beehive wigs and mannered smiles. The '60s. There is hardly any flirting. As if one tried to smell romance in pure oxygen.

And we end up here, in the last resort, where we meet, we who are seekers after all colors and sizes, and bound to fail. Hardly anyone is absent. And those who are may still come. This is our sanctuary. It is nourished exclusively by the energy of love. Stimulants, drugs, medicines, and similar things are unacceptable here. I enjoy myself. It is like coming home from Mars. I swim in eroticism and spread it around. Today (it is already a new day) the interior is padded with pink viscose. Unnaturally large lipsticks slowly melt in the corners. We sit leaning against the wall, Tiziana, I, and the others. Our legs roll about with abandon on the soft dark blue plush carpet. Feeling self-assured, I indulge myself in giving my full attention to numerous beautiful women. I let my warm words drop into their laps. I tease them, give them what they need most—the rustlings of awakened senses. I do not give myself to them sexually, because love is something I already have. And I do not do it with just anyone.

I suddenly notice that Tiziana is gone. I get struck by a dark foreboding, I crumble like a John made of cards for I know she is betraying me. Everybody, all these people, the whole world is duping me. I leave the club cautiously because I am worried about my reputation. I step into a long corridor. To the left and to the right there are a string of copulating chambers, as disgusting as doctors' surgeries. Each of the curtains are drawn open, the beds empty. As if some puritanical deity has exterminated the debauchees with a single blow. I pass some entrances for personnel. I enter a no-entry zone. I feel a constriction near my heart. When I come close to the last chamber, a double one, I can barely hear the audible moaning of a couple engaged in coitus. Even before being absolutely sure, I know my Tiziana is giving herself to the chief pimp. With extreme caution—he surely has a gun within reach—I peep inside with a half of an eye. I see a part of her back. Now I am absolutely sure she is riding dick. She, who usually likes to cry out with all her might, is unusually quiet. She does not want me to hear her. She shivers under the pressure of accumulated passions like a wild beast caught in a trap. It is clear to me that she finds herself in hitherto untasted depths of ecstasy, and that she is trying to control herself with all the power of her will. The pearls of sweat, however, do not slide down her body. They are far too thick.

The pimp blabbers indifferently nonstop. Like some truck driver or a mechanic. So this is how it is done, you son of a postproletarian bitch. I take a quick look around. I am very much afraid of being seen or hurt. Not a trace of a cry of justified anger: how can you let ordure like this be spread on your Carniolan fields! I subdue my wish to escape. I can physically feel, with my appendix or something, that they are close to climax. Then I can stand it no more. Just as, like a shadow, I am slowly going away, I hear the pimp's voice:

"Ahh, I'm coming!"

And then, "Oops! I think some cum dripped into you." Then he immediately changes the topic and starts talking about something terribly banal.

I am overcome by fear. I run away as if Satan were after me.

A rhetorical question keeps pecking at my neck: Just where have I gone wrong?

Translated by IRENA ZORKO

ANDREJ MOROVIČ

Under the Surface

MOJCA KUMERDEJ

"$\boldsymbol{a}$re you sure you aren't coming swimming with me?" he asked me as he was walking across the lakeside gravel into the cold water.

"You know I'm not.... I don't like swimming," I replied, just as I do every time he asks me. As if he had forgotten, or else he does it because he doesn't want to remember.

You will never know the real reason. I will never tell you. For us to spend the third summer, our summer together, by ourselves, without anyone interrupting us, there had to be a sacrifice. On that early July afternoon not only did I see everything, but I didn't do anything—and by doing so did everything. It was probably fate that I went to the house from the beach because I was feeling sick all morning and wanted to throw up. Perhaps I was reading, perhaps not; I probably wasn't doing anything, except walking around the house and going out onto the terrace a few times. I saw you playing on the beach, you and the little one with her long curly hair. It isn't true that I didn't think about what happened later that afternoon, that I didn't even wish for it. I have never cared much about children, I haven't even thought about them, and it only seemed that we would have one—just because in a relationship between two people who love each other this usually happens. I probably wouldn't even think about that seriously if I hadn't seen that woman calculatedly moving around you, flattering you, purposely fixing her hair when speaking to you, the corners of her lips trembling before uttering a word, biting and—it seemed, incidentally, but in fact it was meanly and calculatedly—licking her lower lip, and your look becoming moist and frozen.

That's when I knew I had to take action. After all she was more attractive than me, and she had the ability to release a kind of a warm magnetic field around her, which I simply can't do. And that's how it happened. When for the first time you put your hand on my stomach I knew I had you, and that's when I decided to have you forever, wholly and completely, without intermediary, disturbing elements that could jeopardize our love.

But when the little one came along, you changed, and above all you stopped looking at me the way you used to. Not anymore as a lover but as the mother of your child. As the mother of a little one who was changing from a baby into a girl, and then more and more, I noticed, into a little woman. Every time you returned home you first hugged the little one, played with her honey-colored hair, kissed her on the cheeks, and only then was it my turn. And the first months the little one was crying, she was crying an indescribable amount, so much so that at that time I already thought something should be done. She was waking me every night with her piercing screams, and I had to keep getting up to try to silence her, while you rarely got up because you needed to have your sleep, whereas I didn't because I was staying at home with her. In order to take care of her. In order to take care of your child. Of your favorite sweetheart, as you often put it, not even noticing how it hurt me. She knew all too well that she came first, that you loved her more than you loved me. Often I noticed a mocking smile in her big bright eyes when you hugged her while I was waiting my turn. The little one could be mean, very mean and conspiratorial. She kept making up totally untrue things: like, for example, that she didn't get the food that she wanted that day, or that I had promised to her the day before, and that I slapped her a few times because she didn't obey me at the shopping center when she tore herself away from my arms only to attract attention. The employees had to search for her using the loudspeaker, and the shop assistants were rummaging and poking about among the coat hangers together with me, until they finally found her in the sportswear department. She was laughing in my face, as if to say, Look how many people were looking for me, everyone wanted to find me, including you, who don't have anyone in the world who would care for you. And then, at that moment when they brought her to me, I didn't really slap her but I held her more tightly and patted her thick hair, and she screamed as if it hurt. But it didn't. I was the one feeling pain because she embarrassed me, just like so many times before; all eyes were turned toward me: how did I bring her up so badly, what kind of a mother was I, and things like that I was reading in their looks. And you, at home, weren't furious with her but with me, for letting her out of my sight, for allowing your child to tear away from mother's safe arms.

She did this lots of times only to be at the center of attention. When friends came over to visit, she would sit in the armchair, cross her legs, and then like a little woman ask what for a child were rather unusual questions, even about sex. Oh, how everyone adored her; this one will be the true destroyer of men, she will hold them at bay, even now you can tell how smart she is and more than that, it's clear she will be a real beauty. Smart and beautiful, the guests said while looking at you. Her father's daughter, they must have thought, thank God she doesn't take as much after her mother. She has his blue-greenish eyes, his big lips and disarming smile with which she can achieve everything, his remarkable skill in communicating. Surely several men wondered what you had seen in me. Okay, now that we have a child, yes, but what had you seen in me when you were falling in love with me? People are always calculating things, falling in love with people who are as attractive as they are, and are somehow always judging who they aren't pretty and attractive enough for, and who is not worthy of them. But when they looked at us, they probably noticed and thought that he would probably have deserved someone more attractive than me. But no woman in this world would be capable of loving you as much as I do, no woman in this world would be capable of doing what I did—just by doing nothing in that crucial, fatal moment.

When the little one came, everything changed. Our Sundays were no longer like they used to be, when we would lie in bed until noon, with a huge wooden tray on the floor, laden with fruit, whole wheat bread, cheese, and coffee with cardamom. No, just as we started to wake up and you hugged me, the door would open and she would run to us in her nightgown, jump on the bed and hug you. And everything would be over for that Sunday, for that week. Our time was becoming more and more the little one's time, she was the one giving rhythm to our mornings and nights. You didn't want us, as I suggested once, to simply lock ourselves in; you never knew when she'd feel the need to creep from her room into our bedroom. That isn't good, it isn't human, you said, she is still a child and she needs us. That's true, I said, but not every time she feels like it? What about us? She is our daughter, you would look at me sharply every time, reproachfully, as if I didn't love your child enough. Every morning I woke up, felt you beside me and started touching you, I would be looking toward the door in fear, listening carefully and wishing not to hear the tiny steps coming toward our bedroom, the door handle not to turn.

She always managed to steal attention. Even on my birthdays. I had prepared everything carefully, tidied myself, everything was all right, but then, when people came, some with their children too—so it is, if your birthday is in summer and everyone likes being by the barbecue, which is in the garden where children can move around without fear and danger—the little one was once again at the center of attention and interest. And the moment after they gave me presents, they forgot why they had come at all. I mentioned to you that I wanted to celebrate differently, not in the afternoon and with all those children, but in the evening, the two of us together, alone, and we would take the little one to our parents. You were against it both times, as if as to say my birthday was a holiday for the whole family, and that our parents would be insulted if we didn't invite them. I gave in only because I would do anything for you, because I love you as much as I have never loved anyone else, and especially as much as I have never been loved. But you don't know how it is to love someone more than they love you, to know that his touch and squeeze are squeezing someone else harder; while you're willing to give him everything you have, and do anything, in order to give him even what you don't have. And precisely that is what I did for you, and once in my life took what meant the most to me and was, for the fifth year, slipping away from me.

That summer the little one was four and a half years old. It was a very hot summer, like the ones I was once delighted about, like, for instance, the summers that we used to spend on the Adriatic, just the two of us, before the little one was born. But with her arrival some kind of family vacation started, with our friends and their children. The couple we spent July with three years ago also had a child, who was no longer that. She was fifteen years old, tall and slim, even a little taller than I was and with such perfect skin that only some teenagers can have. You think I haven't noticed how she stretched her young, long, and not fully developed body like a puma, how she purred and pouted her lips whenever you asked her something, and when she, seemingly without interest but in fact completely in love, talked to you? About what? I was thinking, when I watched you from a distance so that I couldn't hear the words and saw only the body language, which was unambiguous and clear: we like each other very much. I knew you wouldn't dare do anything, she was only fifteen, she was the daughter of our friends, only a decade older than your daughter. But as I was watching this creature, a growing woman whom you would surely touch in a few years' time, three perhaps, and in different circumstances, and wouldn't just stick to the foolish conversations with her—Whatever can you talk about with a teenager, I ask you!—as long as the conversation is not an excuse to be with her, exactly the way and the amount of time the rules of decency allow, I was discovering more and more the little one in her.

It was probably fate that I stood up that July around noon and went from the beach to the house above it. I don't remember exactly what I did next, probably nothing special other than going out onto the terrace a few times and watching as you talked to the fifteen-year-old while you played with the little one. The next time I looked, you and your sea princess were building sand castles. You were alone, following our friends; the girl had also moved from the beach to the shade.

When I looked through the window the last time, I saw your sunburned body, lying under the open sunshade. The little one was playing in the sand next to you. The inflatable plastic dolphin that you had left close to the surf started to move with the outgoing tide. The little one noticed. When the sea began to cover the dolphin and the first stronger wave started carrying it away, she ran after it. I stepped onto the terrace, and at that moment I wished for exactly what started to happen. You were still sleeping, the little one was wading after the dolphin, trying to grab it, but it was slippery and it kept evading her. I knew: one scream, one loud scream would have woken you up, you'd have leapt after the little one and grabbed her and torn her from the foam that was bubbling on her body. At that moment I saw a chance for things to be the way they used to. Me and you, the two of us alone, and no one to measure the rhythm of our hours, days, nights, our years in the future. It seemed as though everything around me stopped, sounds disappeared, and the light was blindingly white. With eyes partly open, I was watching the scene, and it seems to me I didn't feel anything. No pain, no kind of fear, I was only watching what I thought as things happened. At one moment the little one was clinging to the dolphin's fin handles, and then a big wave tore the inflated animal away from her so that she helplessly let go. I saw her little hands trying to hang on to it, and then her body being sucked into the depths.

I didn't watch anymore. I turned around and went into the house, poured myself a glass of brandy, and fell onto the bed. I shut my eyes, and the world in front of me and behind me darkened. I fell into a dreamless sleep. And when, after a while, I felt a hand and saw the watery eyes of our woman friend, I knew that it had happened. That the story was over. The little one—she hugged me and squeezed me tight—the little one is gone, the woman burst into tears. I got up, dizzy from the brandy and, probably, from the weird sleep, and saw you sitting in the armchair of the living room, wrapped up in a white cover, squeezing the little inflatable dolphin. Our friend was sitting next to you on the sofa beside his fifteen-year-old daughter, who had seen death for the first time in her life. There were some more people in the house, then the policemen and the coroner came. The girl had found her. When she had returned to the beach after lunch, she had seen the little one's body on the surface, face down toward the seabed. As if mad, presumably, you jumped into the sea and tried to revive your sea princess, who had already swum away to different seas, oceans, rivers, and lakes. Yes, I think that although we buried her body, she somehow spread into the waters of the Earth. I sometimes even think that I remember how at the moment when she was trying to hang on to the dolphin with all her might, her eyes met mine, how she saw that I was watching everything but didn't help. That I just let her die.

Not that I didn't feel badly after her death; after all, she was my daughter as well. But in those few months I felt badly because of you, and how you reproached yourself about her death, because you, as sometimes happens, fell asleep on the beach for half an hour just at the wrong time. And you felt guilty on my account as well, the mother of your child whom you didn't protect against death. I was loving, very loving and understanding toward you, I kept persuading you, consoling you that it was an accident, that it wasn't your fault that this happened. It seems to me as if her death became your final commitment to me, although at the same time I know that what you feel for me isn't as much love as the feeling of guilt.

Once, for a moment, I think, you doubted me and asked, You loved her, too, didn't you? Of course, I replied, she was our child. I remember your look, as if you weren't satisfied with the answer and wanted to hear something more.

And I hugged you, snuggled very tightly up to you and started slowly and gently to make love to you. It was Sunday morning and nothing could interrupt us.

You have changed with the little one's death, you're more vulnerable and soft and don't flirt with other women and girls so much anymore. When you carefully mention to me that we should have another, second child, I sadly turn away and say, You know that I can't, it's too painful. You caress me and let me know with a kiss that you understand. But you don't. You will never find out the truth that I don't like swimming because I feel that as soon as I would sink into the water, I would feel her soft honey-colored hair on my skin, her little arms would cling to me and drag me into the depths.

Sometimes I dream about her being taken away by the sea on her blue dolphin and I run after her, then I dream about her and the dolphin grasping me and dragging me to the seabed. I always wake up in terrifying pain from such dreams, which clutch me in a rigid spasm; I can hardly breathe and my heart pounds, and not only singly, for alongside my own I can hear another, smaller heart, beating a little more quickly. I never wake you up. I wait until it goes away, and I go to the bathroom to take a shower. Then I come back, lie down next to you, kiss you with immense love and tightly squeeze myself to you.

Translated by LAURA CUDER TURK

To Serve or Not to Serve

MOHOR HUDEJ

i went to my bar, or rather, café. I went there the same time as every morning. Everything was the same as every other day: it was full of the regulars, each one sitting in the customary chair that was tacitly reserved for him. Old acquaintances in their firmly entrenched positions. Each of them played his role in the bar, and from his respective seat. If someone wanted to replace somebody else, he would just take the seat of someone not there. Occasionally it happened that your seat was taken by an outsider ignorant of the hierarchy, so then you just sat someplace else, not making a fuss. When the owner of the chair you'd taken showed up, you got up, for it wasn't his fault that someone had taken your chair.

Like I said, it was an ordinary day. Everyone sitting in their chairs, my chair empty. From the table nearest the door the usual thing could be heard when I went in. Around Mito's chair, three kids were gathered, some disbelief showing on their faces. Mito was saying, "And then Jesus said to Paul ..."

In the opposite corner, Vojko: "If you need spare parts for a Citroen Diana, it's best to go to the city dump. You'll never get them at that moron's garage. Every time you go there he tells you to come next week. Then there's another possibility...."

The café consisted of three rooms. The bar was in the middle; these conversations were taking place in the room closest to the entrance, and the room where I had my seat was further inside. My seat was the best if you wanted to have a view of the entire bar. Also in that room everybody was in their place, a thing I only noticed when I entered. I sat down. Everybody could see me, and I could see them.

"I don't give a fuck, I'll cut him up for a thousand deutschmarks. I'll tear him open from here to here...." Niko pointed at the stomach of some guy I'd never seen before and then swished enthusiastically up to his chin.

The guy answered, "Czechs are a fucking problem, it can even happen that ..."

Jani across the room was holding the *Sports News* in his hands and expounding, "Even if they lose the rematch they might still advance on goal differential. Unless ..."

I exchanged brief greetings with everyone, so stereotypically that it had ceased to annoy us. A loud discussion had broken out at the bar. The participants were so impassioned they failed to notice me. Their vocal cords straining, each tried to be heard over the others: "These morons shoot down a helicopter and think they're so macho, but nobody thinks like that in Europe. They're just going their own ways slowly toward the postindustrial society, and plurality is common practice. The real postmodern age ..."

Slightly off to the side someone else said, "Apparently the jackpot's two million dollars."

About a year previously, the bar had changed owners, or maybe got its first owner, what the fuck do I know. There was so much talk about it. One of the regulars, a guy with a permanent chair, became the new owner. The radical changes in society had taken their toll.

After the old owner left, the new one, in the general spirit of change, introduced a new regime. A new form of service. Now customers were served at their tables; before they'd had to go to the bar. This novelty was supposed to be more modern, more chic, more for the benefit of the patrons.

That day, the owner was tending the bar. He also had a waiter who worked the other shift. The owner and I couldn't stand each other and hadn't for a long time. It was an organic thing. Our relationship was restricted to a sour formal greeting, so sour its acidity let us both know that we were just shouldering the traditional burden of greeting between people from different walks of life who happen to end up in the same company.

But I had to give him credit: He was a good waiter. Consistent in his logic. You always got what you expected. He made no distinctions between customers. A professional and a know-it-all, we were all patrons to him, or consumers as he liked to say.

He was so good that I felt unable to provoke him; I didn't even try. I could not get out of the obligation of that sour greeting. I hate dead weight! I searched for a flaw in his work, in his service, but he always instinctively knew when he had to come 'round. Every time he would come just as you opened your mouth to summon him, and he always had a plausible excuse ready for being a little slow. In this way he kept the whole café fidgety, or collectively dreamy, even addicted. But I had seen through his little ruse, and he had figured out that I had. Yet he never betrayed his principles. He knew what I expected, and knew how to serve me to keep me quiet and dissatisfied. He knew that I was of the old school in the bar, and that I didn't give a shit about his table service. If I ordered—out of pure malice and to make a point—at the bar, he would place my order in front of me and say, out of pure malice, "I do serve the tables."

He knew I always ordered the same thing, but he never skipped the ritual of modality. Like, "Perhaps the customer would like something else today?" He knew this senseless exchange every morning bothered me, but he would not back off. With an uncanny understanding of my patience, he moved along the borderline that kept our hostile relationship within the sphere of nonviolent words and actions. In this respect, he was stronger than me, and he gloated and with his taunts rubbed my nose in his superiority.

That day was no different. As usual, he came up and asked obsequiously, "May I take your order, please?"

I likewise took a jab at his patience: "The usual."

He never dropped below the level at which we still had some kind of respect for each other, to ask, "What's that, the usual?" No, every time he would say, clearly because this was more provocative, more likely to cut me to the quick, "A coffee with milk, right?"

Ordinarily I would answer in a conciliatory fashion, in a tone that made service possible, "Yeah."

My voice betrayed my thoughts. If I were discussing this with someone I would've said, "Why should I screw around with him?"

That day was, as I have now mentioned a number of times, ordinary. Everything bordered on stereotype. In the split second before I stereotypically served his service back to him, I had a flash of insight:

"Damn, he gets off on stereotype!"

He was waiting for me to say what I was supposed to say. I said, "Yeah."

Adding in the same breath: "And ..."

He halted. I raised my eyes, and for the first time we actually made eye contact. We could have established a rapport. He let slip, in an unusually sharp tone: "And?"

Now we had crossed over. I inhaled. There wasn't enough oxygen, I needed gasses of a different sort: "And, and, and ... And nothing." I looked at him. If a guy is working he has no time to screw around.

"Tell me if you want something else, I'm waiting," he said.

"Nothing. *Niente. Nada.* Get it?"

Briefly, he smiled. Most likely at my multilingual reply. God forbid, although that's the way I demagogically interpreted it since it came in handy.

"What are you grinning at? What's your problem? Huh? Fuck this shit!"

"Look here, if you're looking to pick a fight you've got the wrong guy," he said it as a warning, making me think he'd immediately call the cops if anything went wrong. It's a challenge. I thought, this son of a bitch wouldn't even defend himself if I kicked his ass. He'd just take it. Jesus fucking Christ.

I could not—and would not—sail back into more peaceful waters. I said, enjoying the thrill of the fight, "Hey, don't screw with me! I'm in a bad mood today, you hear? You . . ."

I ventured, "You chicken shit."

The people around us had noticed there was a quarrel going on. There was a sudden hush. "Is there a storm brewing?"

My last words had been heard by all. They exchanged puzzled glances. "What's with those two?"

Now they were waiting. Some of them were on my side, the others on his. Depending on whom they hated more. The fact that they hated us both was unmistakable. We liked one another only if we happened to meet in some other bar where we were not regular guests.

One of those who hated me more than him said, "What's the matter with you? Have you lost your mind?"

That was weird. Different than it should have been. Usually, they're all quiet, or else they all expect someone else to step in. Most likely Mito. Nobody likes to get mixed up in anything. Why make people mad without a reason? The lone voice encouraged the others to interfere and start making peace. They shouldn't have tried to pacify me. I automatically linked them with him. Things had gone too far.

"He's fucking with me, don't you get it?" I yelled at the guy responsible for the wave of mollification. I looked out the window and then turned my eyes to the ceiling.

"Huh? Don't you see? What the fuck! Are you all deaf and blind? And mute? Holy shit! Can't you see all this moron cares about is robbing us blind with that fucking snippy face of his?" I asked nervously. I looked at him: "Just counting the euros. Ain't that so? You prick!"

Someone said, "Look, if you're in a bad mood, don't bring it in here!"

"What fucking bad mood! Why the fuck shouldn't I be in a bad mood? All we do is sit here, each of us with his own theory of why we're just sitting, and why we're sitting here, and who's to blame. We quarrel, and in the end we part in peace. Everyone has his own opinion, and it's right that we should be different. In between we call this son of a bitch to get us a beer or two, and it's so nice when this son of a bitch serves us with his tray. We sit on these soft seats until our asses hurt from all the comfort.... And this son of a bitch would even bring us footstools so our little tushes could be even more comfortable, so we'd be even more drowsy, and then peanuts and a prick on a plate! What the fuck are you staring at, you faggot! You motherfucker!"

I concluded by fixing him with my eyes in a way that is not appropriate for anyone.

He continued to look at me. He was probably simply unable to believe his eyes and ears. He was tapping his tray against his thigh. Apparently in time with his pulse. Pretty unhurried. He obviously still derived calmness from having some of the guys on his side. Or was it shock?

"Gimme that fucking tray!" I yelled at him as soon as I'd recovered my breath.

"Why?" he asked as though nothing had happened.

"So that I can fling it through your fucking window," I told him calmly, in his tone of voice and at his volume.

"Why?" he asked as stupidly as possible.

All I could say was, "Well, because you're an idiot, and because this tray's here in this bar so that it can be flung through the fucking window."

He gripped the tray tighter and shuddered a moment. I leapt toward him. He got scared and let go of the tray. I carried out my threat with a slight variation. I threw the tray at the row of glasses above the bar. It produced a crash a window could not have rivaled.

Someone said, "Fuck!"

And someone else: "Oh, fuck!"

I'm done with these morons, I thought, feeling relieved. Everybody was now looking at the impact of my action. When they turned to look at me, I told them, "Go fuck yourselves!"

I walked out, kicking at a glass that rolled under my feet. Outside, I regretted not having spit too.

I felt calm, relaxed as never before. I immediately found my car keys. As I was unlocking my car, the owner I had assaulted came running out of the bar.

"What? You want a piece of me?"

I took a few steps toward him, but all he wanted was to tell me meekly, "I don't know, I'm sorry. I have no idea what upset you so much. Come back again, come on. Tomorrow, when you've calmed down. I'm sorry if there was something wrong. I'm sorry."

Astounded, I stared at him. Could he possibly be so fucking cynical? Is he serious? I got in my car and thought: Could I possibly have been wrong?

Translated by TAMARA M. SOBAN

On Angels

ANDREJ E. SKUBIČ

> After the lamentation had gone on for hundreds and hundreds
> of whatever the angels use for time, an angel proposed that
> lamentation be the function of angels eternally, as adoration was
> formerly. The mode of lamentation would be silence, in contrast
> to the unceasing chanting of Glorias that had been their former
> employment. But it is not in the nature of angels to be silent.
> —DONALD BARTHELME, *On Angels*

"'Scuse me, got any change?"

Just a vacant stare, really nothing but a vacant stare, like some half-frozen reptile, some Gila monster, then he goes the fuck away 'round the corner, not even a Sorry, buddy. He just split, the little dork. Like the cunt didn't even see me.

"Have a nice day," I say.

He doesn't give a shit. And I don't give a shit either. About him. I don't give a shit. My head's already buzzing. On top of everything else. Anyway, something tells me this cash should be enough. Something tells me.

Yeah, it should be enough. And we got a bottle of liquor, hardly started. Three-quarters full, enough for a decent start to the evening. And enough cash for a bottle of wine at least. Salé has had a skinfull already anyway and can't manage much more. He'll just get more aggressive if he starts knocking it back. There'll be time. Time to get back to the old sugar warehouse, and at least there'll be something happening. We've been somehow down recently. But at least we've got enough to liven things up until Gogi comes with his bunch, they're sure to have collected something. Then things'll brighten up. So we won't be just a bunch of long faces.

But I ask you, these little brats. These fucking little brats. No respect for their elders. None at all. I know what they're like. Before you know it, they're 'round the corner with their hand out. I know what they're like, the little runts.

These runts, I see 'em panhandling—I mean I can hardly believe it. Spoiled brats, you can see straight away they don't need it at all. They're, I dunno, they're most likely just bumming a phone card or something. Or, what do I know, some fucking smack. That poison. 'Cause they've already blown what their folks gave 'em. They take the money right from under the nose of someone who at least knows how to use it. I'll have to have a serious talk with one of 'em sometime. Wave a broken bottle in his mug till he's shitting himself, then break his skull open. So he sees this is a serious business. Just once, for a change.

Veko's sitting on the wall next to Salé and Marjeta, looking edgy. His only aim is not to sober up. He's slumped there on the wall, holding his head in his hands. Totally out of it, totally gone. We were in the same class at primary school. This is the third day in a row. He's from a different planet. Acting in a different movie. I don't know what keeps him going.

I look up. Night's coming on. Late spring, days are already quite long, but cold. Need to get into the warmth. At least somewhere inside, out of the wind. I don't know how Veko stands it. Veko got used to different things. I look at him again, still slumped there, hasn't moved an inch.

What keeps him going? We weren't even that close at school. I was into sports back then, he was more the nerdy type. An egghead. Then, in secondary school, I went totally off the tracks, but he worked his way through grammar school, university, then somehow seemed to make it: he tells me he's doing something like writing novels. Doing some freelance editing. Got a nice apartment, a wife and a kid. One day he bumped into me near my stakeout, down by Hrvaski Square.

I didn't even recognize him. But *he* recognized me. Hmm. Who'd have thought it?

I turn back toward my buddies, Salé and Marjeta, but I'm looking at Veko. He looks completely different than he did then, the first time for twenty years. Different, he looks like someone cleaned the underside of a car with him.

Then, he was wearing clean, smart jeans, a jacket, had a nice leather briefcase, eyeglasses on his nose. Classmates twenty years ago. He looks at me and smiles and says, "So you've ended up like this." Yeah, he looks so different. "What do you mean 'like this'?" "Come on," he says, a bit timid, "don't get fucking worked up, I'll buy you a beer in a bar. You can tell me all about it. How you ended up like this." "What the hell," I say, "okay." How did I know what he actually wanted from me—and who really gives a rat's ass what he wants—if he's paying for a beer? You don't often get offers like that. So he paid, and not just one. Then I saw what he was really after.

It was very simple: the guy just wanted a good excuse to get totally loaded, yeah, just that. Dead drunk. That's all he needed. Not to talk. To be honest, he was one of the most boring guys you could wish for, really. Wife, kids. These books of his, had I read any? The fuck I had. Work, blah blah. But he had the cash, no shortage of that. We hit the sauce like two bloody sailors—no, what am I saying?—like two lords. Like lords, we first had beers, then some kind of brandy chaser. He was on brandy. Then a wine, then a gin, then back to the beer, then more hard liquor. Christ, he looked so rough I thought I was gonna have to call an ambulance, get his stomach pumped and all that, but there was no need. He woke up next morning with Marjeta, Salé, and me in the air raid shelter, still drunk as a skunk, no idea where he was. But first, before he figured out what was going on, he asked if there was a drop of liquor handy.

He drank with us for three days, slept in the old sugar place or the shelter, whichever place we dragged ourselves to. Didn't go home once. As if he wanted to hide there with his bottles—then it was all okay, brandy and vodka. He soon went through all his money, that didn't take long. Then he relied on us looking after him. Just as long as he didn't sober up. 'Cause if he was sober, he'd have to go home. Home to the wife and brat. And that'd be hard, that *will be* hard, to explain nicely where all that moolah's gone, and where mister has been, and where he lost those fucking eyeglasses that gave a touch of class to his flushed face that first day. He didn't want to go panhandling with us, he was too high and mighty for that. But what the hell, we didn't take it the wrong way. After all, the guy had spent a fortune on us in a couple of days, eating and drinking in a bar, not on a bench. A real gentleman, after all.

Then for a good two months there was no sign of him—his wife probably had him under lock and key. Two months. But then, out the blue, who should turn up at Hrvaski Square again but Veko. Only this time he wasn't hiding why he had really come. He had a carrier in his hand with three bottles of red wine. He grinned as soon as he saw us, Salé, Gogi, and me. Well, that time he hung around for four whole days. Then for almost six months neither hide nor hair of him. He was working, being creative. Then two days ago, here he is again, up to his old tricks. With a carrier bag and a full wallet. And full of some tale about how he's written some novel. I'd really like to see this novel of his, to see what's going through this person's head. At a quick guess, I'd say not a lot. Yesterday we were knocking back the red, and he puked up some purple muck behind the benches. Then we were on white wine, better for the stomach, he said. Then gin, which is certainly the best for the stomach, especially in great quantities, and it does wonders for the skin and eyesight. Essential oils, he explained, essential fucking oils, as he slithered down across the bench. He woke up with his eyesight no better and his

ANDREJ E. SKUBIČ

wallet the worse for wear, disappointed in the gin. Then it was back to the old routine, us panhandling, him to the store, all of us happy. And now he's sitting there, almost shitting himself that he's gonna come out of it too quickly.

"We're heading over to the sugar place," I say, when I get to them, and I'm looking through my pockets. I've got the last half-hour's takings in there; they rustle nicely.

"Yeah, it's getting cold," says Marjeta, kind of quiet, already a bit out of it. And yeah, it is getting cold. Maybe I should lend her my jacket. If I was a gentleman.

I'm no gentleman.

"Got enough?" asks Salé, holding the brandy bottle as if he's trying to work out whether it's safe to take another slug, without it running out. He seems kind of nervous, shuffling, he's cold as well. Only Veko isn't, no, not him, because he's got an anorak, a lovely warm anorak, though it's a bit messy from the wine. Yesterday's. Wife won't be too pleased.

"It'll be enough."

A dance across the street. Or rather, Salé is dancing, we're walking normally, he's starting to feel like a king, why should he worry about cars? Veko looks different, too, more playful. The prospect of a new bottle does that to you. Maybe it'll all turn out okay. He dances along behind Salé, wanting to tell him something, his writer's mop flapping in the air. Yep, still talking about the fucking Lithuanian plains. Some time ago he went with some writers on some kind of reading tour of Lithuania, and he was lecturing us yesterday on the phenomenal capacity of the local women to hold their vodka.

"This hill of crosses," he rambles, "this hill of crosses is something else, it's totally weird. You should go there and see it."

"What crosses, for fuck's sake?" reacts Salé, looking at him suspiciously, thinking that perhaps he's bugging him, hassling him. At one time Salé was supposed to go and study theology, his folks had him down for a priest. But nothing came of it, other than that he toasts the Virgin Mary every day. Anyway. "What crosses?"

"There's this little hill, well, not really a hill, a sort of fucking mound, with about a million crosses standing on it. I mean, every size, from massive, nine-foot-high things to others a few inches high, dangling on chains from the big ones, it's littered with them, all swinging. All jingling there in the wind, in the middle of nowhere, the asshole of the universe, nothing but fields for miles around, a million crosses, and the wind blowing like crazy."

"So what?" says Salé, trying to picture it, but it's hard work he's given himself, however spiritual he is.

"I mean—it's creepy, you know, real scary," says Veko, warming to his theme. "When you hear this jingling ..."

"And what were *you* doing?" I ask, just to razz him a little. But it doesn't work, Veko's just happy that someone's paying some attention to his yarn.

"Me," he says, "I was thinking how it would be to get that gorgeous Lithuanian interpreter on her own somewhere among those crosses, and give her one, you know, T-shirt off, pants down, and get stuck in the middle of all those crosses, screw her right there among all those crosses jingling around us."

"You what?" rages Salé. *"You'd fuck among the crosses?"*

"Yeah, and how!" Veko carries on, not seeing what danger he's getting into. "I'd screw her until the saints appeared."

"You're fucking sick, you!" Salé yells. Now all his deeper inclinations are aroused. *"You wanted to fuck among the crosses? You really offend me, you cunt, you really offend me!"*

How ridiculous. I'm thinking, Where's this coming from, Salé? Where did you read that? In some tabloid that somebody left on the bench? Offend you? Who are you bullshitting, anyways? Marjeta's not listening.

She gapes at the walls of the children's hospital as we walk past. Why is Salé so bothered about some crosses? Probably because Veko is talking so much. More than him.

Marjeta gapes at the walls of the children's hospital. She's always gaping at them. Five times a day, for fuck's sake, she goes past and stares. As if it might make made any difference to her. Today, bloodshot and slovenly as she is, she wouldn't even get her foot past reception, they'd turn her straight round and say, "Out, madam." Even if she smartened herself up a bit, with that makeup she carries in that fucking handbag of hers. There's nothing else in there beside the makeup worth mentioning, apart from a pullover. As if she thought a dab of lipstick could make her into a lady. Not that I've got anything against it. She'd look a tiny bit better, raise our beauty rating somewhat, though her what used to be a punk hairdo doesn't help matters much. She's almost forty, but she still nurtures some image from the late '70s.

I don't know what it was, exactly. I don't know why women love confiding in me all the time, for I always forget. But it must be something to do with the way I look that makes them confide in me, a gentle type. She was married, some guy took her on, even though she had an illegitimate daughter, she was a bit of a party girl, enjoyed a good time. Then she had a son with this husband. A happy little family. Problem was, she still enjoyed a good time, partying and that. And that's what they must have argued about all the time, her being a drunken mother and so on. Anyway, one time, quite wasted, she was flying down the stairs, rushing to get her daughter to day care, after she'd just gotten home from some all-night bender. She was pulling her daughter by the hand. Nothing bad happened to her, a couple of bumps, but her little girl banged her head on the edge of a step. They had her inside this building, the children's hospital, for about a month, and then that was it, g'bye. Her husband kicked her out and took their son. Marjeta moved into the park. An educational tale.

We stop in front of a shop and send Marjeta in. Occupy her a bit, so she doesn't think about other things too much. Salé and Veko are still talking about those crosses—fuck them both, they can't seem to help it.

"So you wanted to screw her, did you? Give her a good old screw," Salé is saying. "You ever really had a screw? I mean, look at you!"

It seems as if the whole thing is getting on Veko's nerves, he regrets having said anything, especially the bit about screwing. He'd like to turn the conversation in some other direction. Redirect it a bit, at least.

"This is the other weird thing," he says, his bottom lip trembling a little, and maybe he's gonna start crying now. "The whole time we were there it was boiling hot. I mean, Lithuania, Vilnius, I thought, the North, you know, but it felt like we'd gone to Greece, middle of the spring." No, he's not gonna cry, he's just a bit worked up, it's all nerves, nerves and waiting for what Marjeta's gonna buy. "But when we got to these crosses, that was even further north, and nearer the sea, the wind was absolutely freezing. It was like a knife there, fucking Jesus, an icy wind among the crosses. It came from the Baltic, straight across from that cold icy water. It went right through our clothes. Fucking freezing by those crosses."

I shuddered, don't know why I remembered it just then, maybe the freezing and all that. I remembered a real strange dream, that I was dead.

I dreamed that I suddenly sat upright in my sleep, and I knew something was terribly wrong. There was this strange feeling in the air, that something was seriously wrong, but I didn't know exactly what—the air seemed somehow heavy, I had a lump in my throat, I knew something final had happened. I knew this was fucking it. I don't know if a person always knows at a moment like that with such certainty. That it's over. I touched my neck—it was cold, my muscles and things were all limp. Like a sagging rope. My skin—rough, but slippery, disgusting. Like touching a corpse.

When I got up, I peeled myself off Tadeja's skin like a Band-Aid—
zzzip. The skin on my hip was almost burning from the cold. Oh god, I
thought, she's here too. Who'd have thought? She was sleeping, so she
had no idea. Tadeja. How could you touch a corpse like that in bed?
Tadeja. Hmm? You kept on sleeping, trusting, soft, at my mercy, or
mercilessness. You'd not even dreamed that you'd been in bed the whole
time with a corpse, who was gripping the edge of the quilt, totally useless, while his digestive juices slowly dissolved his stomach from within.
And the blood in his veins curdled. What a pig. Disgusting. How, for
fuck's sake?

I lurched out the room to the bathroom, to look at myself in the
mirror. Is that me? 'Course it is. There's nothing so very unusual to see.
I've always been like that, nothing special. Look. I put my face close to the
glass, so I was almost touching it with my schnozz. Why am I so pale?
'Cept for the blue-red circles under my eyes, swollen like I've been cutting
onions. Eyes? Looks as if the whites have gone darker and transparent,
like dark gray jelly, crisscrossed with dark reddish veins, the color running through transparent glass. Fuck. Like some drifting jelly fish. I'm
dead. I must get away so Tadeja doesn't see me like this, go and join the
angels.

I woke and sat up with a start, a lump in my throat, my tongue as
dry as a two-by-four, the sour aftertaste of cheap wine, dying for a piss.
The sound of breathing in the room. Outside on the street silence, not
a car. Oh, fuck. Fuck.

Marjeta comes from the shop and we go toward the old sugar warehouse. I can't speak. At least nothing that'd make any sense—that brandy
from earlier has got to me, really got to me, maybe too much. It's a real
bummer when that happens. But it's not too bad, you've just got to wait
a bit for your liver to do its stuff. Our livers work for us. Better to say
nothing, keep my yap shut. In any case, Veko and Salé are saying enough
for all of us.

"Where the fuck are Gogi and the others?" says Salé. We're sitting in our space, he's sick of listening to Veko. Marjeta and I are real quiet. We may run out of booze after the two bottles, and then we'll do what, just stare at each other, or what?

"Maybe Gogi'll have more moolah than you think," I say, just like that, as if it doesn't matter what I say. Though the next moment I regret it. Sometimes you can say too much. Yeah, it's better to say nothing, like a real corpse.

"Why?" asks Salé. "What money?"

"Gogi's supposedly got some job, from those three guys," I say, fuck it, might as well go the limit, don't know why Gogi goes 'round telling folks. Veko's staring into space, he's no idea what I'm on about, but Salé looks annoyed. "He's hefty enough for a job like that. These guys said they'd take him with them to get some protection money."

Salé grins.

"Protection? Gogi? And he goes around shouting his mouth off to everyone?"

Marjeta gets up, swaying a bit. She's also pretty far gone, she started so early. Ever since Veko came along, the drinking starts even earlier than usual. She goes toward the mattress in the far corner, where it's darker. I just shrug.

"None of us are going to say anything to anyone. If we don't stick together, who will?"

"Oh yes, we'd really trust you," says Salé with a smirk. "You'd sell your mother for a large bottle of brandy."

I shrug. I fucking well shrug, though he gets on my nerves, my motherfucking nerves. What does he know about me? If anyone'd sell their mother for a large bottle of brandy it's him, and what I told him probably isn't safe, he'll probably go blabbing it around. No one trusts him like they do me. But he's bigger, like a barn door. That's what gets to him—he's bigger and stronger than Gogi, yet it's Gogi they ask. And I know why. 'Cause Gogi's more normal and reliable, and Salé's a fucking psychopath.

"I wouldn't take less than two large bottles," I say.

And we carry on drinking.

We drink, time passes, my vision starts to get a bit blurred, which isn't good. It's certainly not good. I've not eaten enough today. Just a sandwich. We didn't go anywhere, not even for soup. It's nice to have soup sometimes, but now that Veko's here, we never seem to get 'round to it. Maybe I should go on my own. Leave them for a couple of hours, let 'em do what they want. But now it's far too late, and we've no money left. What now? I've got to take care of this hole in my stomach. I can't drink any more, or I'll keel over. That'd be an undignified end to the evening and I don't want that. But how, if we're passing this bottle 'round? Veko's rambling on again, I find it hard to follow what he's on about, my ears seem as if they're sort of clogged or swollen. Marjeta's sitting on the mattress at the back, just listening, still awake. She's not drinking, she's smart.

I get up. I sway a bit as well, but it's not too bad. I'd like to bet Veko couldn't stand up at all now. Don't look at me so questioning now, buddy, you've heard enough stories today for your next novel, you motherfucker.

I stagger back toward the mattress and Marjeta. She looks at me, but doesn't speak. I know she likes it. I'm not making anything up here. I mean she likes a bit of company. So she doesn't just sit on her own at the back. Not 'cause it's me. We'll be on our own a bit, away from those two psychos. Two reasonable people who can confide in each other. Though it doesn't look too promising at the moment. When I sit down next to her it feels like bliss—the soft mattress. Shame she's over there in the corner—that's where I'd like to be. Not to worry, I can lean on the wall. Next to her. Our shoulders touching.

Tadeja. Shit, I just remembered your skin, that I peeled off me in my dream, I mean. . . . It seemed so crazy, it could be real.

You said then that you could never marry me, not even in a moment of craziness. It was true what you said. That I wasn't fit to live with anyone, that the six months I stayed in your one-room apartment was the worst possible fuck-up. Like having a randy tom cat the whole time. An utter waste of time. I couldn't agree more. Even if this comparison, with a tom cat I mean, seemed a bit bizarre. I wasn't horny at all, not once in the whole six months. Not that there weren't any opportunities, there were a lot of likely girls around, and I was young and tasty. You said it was no way to live, one party after another, day after day, never knowing if I was going to come home alive and unharmed, or if you'd have to come looking for me at the precinct or the hospital. I said to you, You're quite right, it is no way to live at all, feeling guilty 24/7, trying to work out whether to call you to see if you're going to join me, when I know you won't want to, and that you could have some girl friend of your own, for fuck's sake, to go out with now and again, let go a bit and enjoy yourself, and then come home in a good mood, not uptight like some fucking nun, and hold onto me like you did at the beginning, do you remember how it was? Yeah, and then your old man says to me one day, he's known me since I was a kid, he stops me on the street and says, "Listen you, I know you're fucking my daughter, I just want you to know if you hurt her you'll have me to deal with, I'll split your head open; she's still very sensitive on account of her brother." You never once said what had actually gone on with this mysterious brother of yours. I asked your pop, "Wouldn't it seem sad to you if your daughter had a boyfriend who didn't hurt her only 'cause he's afraid of you?" "'Course," he said, "but it's still better than if he hurts her just like that." You held onto me when we did it for the first time in your apartment.

"Marjeta," I say and clear my throat, I'm a bit tongue-tied, but it'll be alright, that's how it is, just clearing my throat, that's all it was, nothing else. When we did it the first time.

"Uh," says Marjeta, it seems as if she's barely looking.

"Marjeta, what was it like when you did it for the first time?"

She's totally silent for a few moments.

"When I what?"

Our first time, you held onto me and said you liked *bad* boys like me. You said then you liked boys like that.

"The first time you fucked," I say, and lick my lips, they are bitter, dry and rough.

"The first time I what?" says Marjeta. It's a real tough combination, drinking all day, then questions like this, like we're in some sort of therapy group.

"You know, when you first slept with a guy."

"Oh," says Marjeta and starts thinking hard. She says nothing for a while. I begin to wonder what she's thinking. Probably thinking how to tell me, in some very special, not too ordinary way, to fuck off. Nosey motherfucker. Questions like this. What sort of questions are these?

"*I sveikatà!*" calls Veko, summoning us, waving the bottle of brandy in our direction. Fuck him and his foreign languages, he's been bugging us with this for two days now. No good'll come of it, he doesn't know where he's heading. Salé has had enough of his bullshit. He's kind of allergic to foreign languages.

"The first time," says Marjeta out of the blue, startling me a bit, 'cause I was looking at the other two and I'd almost forgotten that I'd asked anything. "The first time was basically rape." The strangeness, the oddness of that sentence suddenly hits me so hard I'm confused. I turn toward her, with a sudden feeling I've a lump in my throat. Marjeta's voice is strange, maybe 'cause she's so plastered, she's not speaking very clearly, but you can understand what she's saying, understand all too well.

"What do you mean, rape?" You can tell me, Marjeta. I'm a person you can trust.

She sighs.

"It was at some party," she says. "I'd been going out with the guy for a week. I was fifteen. I'd been drinking like a fish...."

So Marjeta knew then already what her mission in life was.

"There was nothing I could do. Next day, I couldn't even bear to look at him."

Salé's got Veko by the throat. It takes a while for me, you know, to become aware of this, my consciousness is full of Marjeta and what she's saying, and it's hard to divert my attention elsewhere. I should probably say something, get in between them. Maybe tell them to cut it out. Maybe I should say to Marjeta that we should tell 'em to *stop*, because Salé, he suddenly gives him one right in the chops, punches him right in the chops, and Veko's teeth are in an instant all red, wet and red. Veko shouts, but Salé's got him by the throat. You won't get away now, Veko, you've had it now.

"I told you to stop bullshitting me," says Salé, and lands another one on him. I stare at them, but can't speak, my throat's so tight.

"The second time," says Marjeta, paying no attention to those two and just carrying on as if she's in a world of her own, "the second time, was when I did ... when I got ..." She doesn't say what and there's no need. I know what. We all do. She was past seventeen then, I seem to remember. Though I didn't know here then. "Only that time I didn't even know," says Marjeta, though she still hasn't finished her last sentence, she just leaves it, disregarded. "I was so drunk at that party I flaked out in another room and in the morning I woke up with my knickers half down, and the guys were all sniggering meaningfully, and no one wanted to even hint which of them actually had."

Her voice is real strange, I'm not imagining it, it really is, like she's going to burst out crying any minute. What's all this about? Salé suddenly shoves Veko toward the wall, he goes flying, but he doesn't get to the wall 'cause it's too far, there are things scattered on the floor, he trips and falls backward, landing on his elbows and yelling like a stuck pig. Salé goes after him, is already over him, and gives him one hell of a kick in the back. I look at them numbly, something ought to be said, I should say something, I really ought, after all, Veko was at school with me, I've got some responsibility to a classmate. I can't let him be slaughtered like this.

I clumsily raise myself against the wall and push myself into a sitting position. I carefully turn toward Marjeta.

"Those two've got no idea," I say and nod toward them, Veko lying there and Salé still at it, dancing 'round him, getting kicks in wherever he can. Hard kicks. Marjeta doesn't reply. Her eyes are almost closed, between her lashes you can just see a hint of white wetness, she probably can't see anything. She's not asleep, is she? She can't be asleep. She was talking to me. Telling me about it. Telling me an interesting story, an experience. Telling it very well, I thought.

There's shouting from underneath the window. Some guy's walking along the street and howling.

"Clementina!" he yells like an animal. "Clementi-i-ina-a-a!"

I'm suddenly gripped by a strange urge to be gentle. I'm feeling so gentle. Salé's leaning over Veko, he's lifting Veko's head and smashing his fist into his mouth, Veko's mug is all bloody, it's becoming a bloody mess, he's looking worse and worse, this Slovenian writer's really going to have something to write about this time. I feel I'd like to be all gentle. Marjeta just says nothing. She's silent.

I carefully put my arm across her shoulder. She doesn't respond. She doesn't speak.

I move slightly so my ass is next to her hip, I move my arm even further across her shoulder, so that I'm actually kind of embracing her, my left arm around her neck, and put my right hand on her knee, on her jeans. She's wearing tight jeans, she's very thin. She's not bloated by alcohol like some. She's holding up well. She's holding up as well as can be expected.

Marjeta puts her head on my shoulder. That's a good sign. Better than violence. Salé's up again, dancing 'round Veko again and kicking him. Veko's not moving at all now, he's not shouting, he's stopped resisting, he seems to think it best if he just waits for it to be over, for Salé to get tired of it. He's probably right. Salé is such a psycho. I stroke her leg with my left hand, let her feel I'm gentle, let her feel I'll protect her, whatever happens I'd never let Salé do anything to her, not to her. I stroke her, her jeans seem rough beneath my fingers, somehow rough. Marjeta's lost in thought, her eyes properly closed now, it's damp beneath them. What can I do?

I stroke her a bit more firmly, squeeze her thigh a little, then let go. No reaction. The feeling I have is quite indescribable, something real soft and heavy is pressing on my head, at the same time everything is cut up inside, the cold is slicing into me, there's an icy draught somewhere 'round my chest, as if that fucking wind from the Baltic was blowing. My hand slips down between Marjeta's legs, where it's warm. I need some warmth, I desperately need some. I'd so like to warm up a bit. I hear Salé panting, he's trying that hard.

I suddenly feel as if Marjeta's finally responding, she's lifted her head from my shoulder, she's grimacing slightly, though her eyes are still closed. I look in her face while I try to get my hand up right between her legs, there where it's warmest, but I can't, she's squeezing her legs together, which I don't like at all.

"No," she says quietly, still with a grimace.

Why not, for fuck's sake?

I don't mean any harm. I'm on your side, Marjeta. If anyone loves you it's me, 'cause I understand so well how it felt when you woke up with your knickers around your knees, and those guys giving each other those looks. What a fucking bummer it must've been. It's good you told me, so I can imagine what it was like and feel bad about it. You felt like dirt, like the last bit of garbage someone chucks in the can, and they can't even be bothered to close the fucking lid properly. Besides which, at that instant you didn't even know a strange thing was growing inside you—anyway, it definitely didn't come into the best hands. For the next four years. How was it when you found out? I really can't imagine what that was like. Why are you moving away? I hold her tighter.

Marjeta suddenly wrenches herself free of me, she has her eyes open now, she looks at me like poison, distrustful. I raise my hands for a moment with surprise, and for some time we glare at each other.

"So what's up now?" I say, sober all of a sudden, as if the brandy has evaporated out of me, there's just me and her, I can feel myself hard inside my pants, oh ho, the old snake's alive and well, not completely past it. Then I lay my hands on her, one on each shoulder, and try to pull her toward me, to hold her. Just to calm her down, for her to know I'll take it slowly, I'll be gentle, she'll enjoy it, I won't do anything to hurt her. But no, she doesn't want to, she pulls away from me. She pulls away, tears herself away, and suddenly slides off the mattress, she's on all fours in front of me, she crawls along the wall, scrambles on all fours toward the door, like some cocker spaniel. Christ, this is weird.

Without thinking, I jump up. Christ, this isn't happening! Where's she going now? She thinks she's just going to fuck off out of the room. Where the fuck to? This is the only space with a bit of warmth. She's still scrambling, looking sideways, toward the door, mad panic in her eyes, as if she's being hunted, as if some horrific monster is fucking well after her, as if someone wants something from her. But who wants anything? In three leaps I'm at the door, I stand in front of it, she's not getting out here. She doesn't even look at me properly, it's as if she can't even see me, though she obviously can, oh yes, she can see me quite easily, 'cause in a moment she changes direction and crawls just as fast toward the opposite wall, then along it, then along the next wall, where there's another door, a door with stairs going up.

"Wait!" I shout, but she doesn't hear, so I take a couple of steps after her. "Marjeta!"

This is crazy, totally stupid, I mean what does it look like? And where does she think she's going? Why doesn't she just give me a couple of minutes, I would only need a couple of minutes, just a couple of lousy minutes, and I'd definitely get her going, I would, no problem, if she'd just give me some time, just give me a chance, just not run away from me. She'd be nice and warm too; she too needs some warmth. Why the fuck is she running away from me? She'd enjoy it so much. She doesn't know what's good for her.

And that's how it goes on. Marjeta crawls toward the door, I call her, I go after her, blood pulsing slowly in my prick, my heart beating faster and faster. Salé's still swaying around Veko's crumpled body, and every so often he takes a run at it and gets a good kick in, Veko lets out a high-pitched sound like a cricket, as if he can't stop himself from groaning softly. This isn't good, this shouldn't be happening, this is bad. Marjeta's scrambling away from me on all fours, though I only want to help her, to make her warm. What the fuck is this? How it could it happen? Let the whole damn fucking universe fuck itself if it wants, but I'm trying hard here, I really am, as much as I can, nobody can say I'm not.

Translated by DAVID LIMON

ANDREJ E. SKUBIČ

On the Boundary Line

JANI VIRK

He knew it would happen some time. He knew very well. But he was only sorry he hadn't brought a knife or a gun. When he went into the village in the evenings, he almost always carried both weapons in his jacket pocket, although he sometimes had trouble from the police for doing so. Across the narrow gravel road leading to his property there stood a cart loaded with lumber; a van drove onto the road behind him and turned on its high beams. He stopped; he couldn't go forward, he couldn't go back. He knew it was them, his neighbors, the five brothers. He opened the door, hopped out of the Jeep, and ran toward the forest; among the dark silhouettes of the trees he saw a way out, but there was no way out. He heard a dog barking in front of him, and a moment later he saw the dog bounding toward him; with his elbow he tried to hit its jaws and managed to evade its bite, but in so doing lost his balance. As he was falling over he heard nervous steps, and an instant later felt a hollow pain in his neck. "Not on the head, not on the head," a voice came from the dark. He knew the voice; he rolled into the fetal position and maneuvered among the kicks and blows from a stick, somebody kicked him in the face with a shoe, warm blood ran over his lips, suddenly he didn't feel the pain any more. As he rolled over the ground he managed to grab a rock, picked it up and threw it at the closest of the brothers. There was a numb heavy sound of a blow and a cry of pain; he flailed around him until he collapsed under the blows and lost consciousness

Even afterward, as he was lying motionless on the ground, they kept kicking and hitting him with sticks, until one of them said, "We must've

killed him, let's stop." In the warm spring night one could hear their gur-
gling breath, the moon was shining onto the unmoving man on the
ground, his face embedded in the sparse grass beside the road. "We killed
him," the male voice repeated and broke into nervous, convulsive laughter. "We killed him, he's gotten what he deserved."

They took hold of his body and dragged him toward the car, placed
him behind the wheel, his head hit the windshield, they closed the door,
he fell across the seats, somewhere far away he perceived a tiny speck of
consciousness that was his consciousness, he saw himself lying covered
in blood across the seats, blood oozing out of his mouth; he inhaled,
through the thick sticky liquid a slender waft of fresh air entered his
lungs, he heard somebody open the trunk of his Jeep, he became aware
of the smell of gasoline and then of burning plastic, from the back of the
rear seats tongues of flame burst with a crackling sound, pink light pen-
etrated through his lids to his eyes, through his memory flashed the image
of his dying father lying trapped under the tractor, vomiting blood during his final breaths. "The fight is over now," he whispered to himself
through his swollen lips. "I'm crossing over, I'll float down the riverbed
of life and sink into the soil." He heard the metallic murmur of the
engine, the brothers were driving back along the road. "The bastards,
they've beaten me," he thought and breathed in the thick, lumpy, suffo-
cating smoke. "Soon I'll be the light of the flame, the fiery grain in the
embrace of darkness, I'll dissolve into the air, rub myself into the smell
of pine needles and the feathers of jackdaws." Before his eyes flashed a
vision of his property, his herd of livestock, his pack of wild dogs, the
graves of his parents at the edge of the forest. "Everything will fall apart,"
he thought, "everything will be overgrown by woods." He stretched his
hand toward the door and hit the glass with the knuckles of his fingers,
lowered his fingers to the door handle, hooked his middle and ring fingers behind it, but didn't have enough strength to open the door; he
gasped for breath in the gooey mixture of blood and thick smoke, he

put his free hand on his belly and tried to raise himself onto his knees, he was choking, and in his desperate gasping for life he managed to gather enough strength to push himself with his knees toward the door and shift the handle with his fingers; he thrust his head against the door and his body lurched into the fresh spring night. With his last remnants of strength, he rolled out of the vehicle, fell onto the sharp gravel and, sinking back into unconsciousness, instinctively rolled into the roadside ditch.

An explosion resounded into the stillness of the night and echoed from the membranes of the hills; pieces of the vehicle flew into the air and fell onto the road and the trees in the moonlight. His body jerked from the explosion, but he didn't regain consciousness; he lay in the ditch on his hip, the blood that had oozed from his mouth was coagulating on his cheeks, from his forehead the warm blood was still slowly dripping across his closed eyelids. He didn't know where he was, he wasn't thinking about who he was, he was floating in matter lighter than water and heavier than air, fiber-like layers, peeled off from huge white pillars, fell like drizzle all around and reassembled themselves into new pillars, everything was in a state of disintegration, there was no living being anywhere, only the murmuring whirlpools of formless life, flakes of bubbling energy, the pure light of a kind of being he didn't know. He heard the voice of his mother, a silent, gentle soothing that he didn't understand, the caressing of her voice, the soft touch of her lips without form, the drizzle of her warm breath without smell. He hovered, light and translucent, flaky white tissue among the changing forms; he was dissolving and being recombined, and yet he remained always the same, always different and always himself in an extendible and indestructible speck of consciousness.

The van drove down the dusty gravel road, bouncing from side to side. Two of the brothers had smashed faces; the rock had crushed the lip of the youngest and knocked out some teeth. Leaning against the window, he whimpered and hissed through his swollen mouth.

"We should've tortured him slowly," he said.

"No," somebody else said. "It's enough we killed him."

"No," somebody else said. "We should've knocked all his teeth out with stones and then done him in slowly."

"No," somebody else said. "We did the right thing. The main thing is, he's dead."

"No," somebody else said. "We should've killed him gradually, bit by bit, we should be torturing him now. We did away with him too fast. Now he's dead and he isn't suffering any more, but our brother will have to put up with the empty spaces between his teeth for the rest of his life."

"And he'll be dead for the rest of his life, which is worse," somebody else said and laughed with a coarse cough.

"What are we going to say back home?" somebody else asked.

"We'll say that he hit our lumber cart and that his Jeep caught fire," somebody else said.

"Yes," somebody else said and laughed heavily, distortedly, "it's not our fault if that is what happened."

"Yes," somebody else said, "it's not our fault. He was asking for it. He'd been bothering us for too long."

When the van stopped at the homestead, the light was still on in the kitchen although it was well after midnight. Two of the brothers grabbed the youngest by the armpits, and they went into the house. In the kitchen the father was sleeping in his wheelchair, and the mother and sister were putting plates on the table. When the mother saw them, she stopped; she noticed the two bloody faces.

"What happened?" she asked.

"A tree fell in the wrong direction and got them," said the oldest.

"Why didn't you bring them home earlier?" she asked.

"It happened when we were almost done," he replied. "It was pitch dark; we didn't know it was that bad. They wanted us to finish. They were still able to help.

"And then we wanted to put out the cart that was on fire," somebody else said. "The neighbor came by and crashed into it."

The father, an old man in his eighties, with red eyes, confused from age and the sleep he'd just woken up from, looked vacantly around. He raised himself in the wheelchair, the metal screeched, everybody looked toward him.

"What happened to him?" he snarled at his sons with a hoarse, rude voice.

"He burned to death," said one of the brothers.

"You didn't help?" asked the old man.

"No," said the oldest.

"You did right," said the old man. "This is what happens to those who stand in our way. It took too long. It's too late for me. You can celebrate." With eyes red from a thick web of capillaries he scanned the room, nobody dared interrupt his look with words. He smiled contemptuously, and then his head drooped on his shoulder and he went back to sleep.

"You killed him," said the mother. "Why don't you tell him that you killed him, it would make him happy."

"We didn't kill him, Mama," said the oldest. "They could lock us up if we killed him, you know. He killed himself, he burned to death and we didn't help him, that's all. I told you, he crashed into our cart, into our lumber. It's all his fault."

"Yes, it's his fault," somebody else said.

She didn't believe them, but it didn't matter. All that mattered was that the young neighbor was dead, and there would be peace for a while.

"Klara, take father to bed," she said to the daughter. "I'll give them some food."

The daughter loosened the safety brake on the wheelchair and pushed her father out of the kitchen. He was snoring, making the sounds of rusty saw teeth sliding loosely along wet wood. Klara hated her father, was afraid of him yet admired him. Although he'd been confined to the wheel-chair for five years, nothing on the farm or in the forest happened without him. He knew every tree, every span of the land, every animal on his property. He knew people, he knew his sons, he knew that—with him being an invalid—they'd rush at him and do away with him if he didn't intimidate and keep them at bay with the story about the gold. Twenty years he'd spent in Australia, he returned in his forties, bought a young girl through an ad, and fathered six children. From abroad he brought back quite a lot of money he'd saved, and he invested it in his property and purchased the neighboring land. Everybody gave in; if necessary, he paid three times more than the land was worth. Only with the old neighbor had there been trouble; no wonder he had been buried by a tractor, his sons had seen the tractor tip over and bury him beneath it, and after that there was trouble only with the young neighbor; no wonder he crashed into a lumber cart, his sons had seen him crash into it.

"They think I'm asleep," he mumbled half-napping, as his daughter was wheeling him out of the kitchen. Thick, brown, nicotine saliva dribbled from his mouth as from a dog's jaws. "They're trembling with fear that I might die without telling them where the lumps of gold are buried, the hyenas! They'll rip my tongue out of my mouth when I die and don't tell them anything," he mumbled through his clenched teeth. He smiled to himself, there were no lumps of gold anywhere, although he kept saying he'd brought them decades ago from Australia and hidden them somewhere on the property. All he had brought was a lump of ore with some glittering traces of gold, and the lump now stood motionless on the mantelpiece like a promise of wealth and power; the sons humbly walked past it, bowing to their father, to the one who knew, to the one who'd bequeath a fortune to them and make them happy.

"Now the road's open," said the oldest son in the kitchen. "We won't have to drive all the way 'round any more."

"Yes," somebody else said, "we'll cut the wires and pull down the barrier."

"We'll shoot his dogs," somebody else said.

"No, we'll poison them," somebody else said.

"We'll slaughter his livestock and sell it," somebody else said.

"We'll level the graves of his parents," somebody else said. "We won't have to put up with them next to us, living or dead."

The mother watched them proudly, her sons. "They've grown into real men," she was thinking. "They're so hard and brave, and yet so tender toward me and their father. God knows they aren't bad, only life up here is hard. God knows they're actually good and humble, but they have some of their father's hot blood in them."

"What do you think, they killed him, right?" he asked Klara, when she wheeled him to the bed. His head rested on his shoulder as if his neck were broken; it gave her the shudders. "He's sleeping and talking," she thought. "He's dead and talking."

"I don't know," she said quietly and thought of the neighbor. She hated him, as her entire family hated him, but she hated him differently. After she had finished primary school down in the valley four years ago, she was never again alone among people she didn't know. She worked on the farm, and only every now and then went to town shopping with her brothers. She saw new faces mostly on TV, they had a satellite dish up on the roof, a huge white disk, and on Saturdays she usually watched programs late into the night, in English, which she could hardly understand. The fresh corpse her father was talking about was familiar to her; she had often watched him, his property was beneath theirs, and although there was a strip of forest along the stream that separated the two farms, she could see his from their barn as if on the palm of her hand. She knew the neighbor's face well, although she never saw him right up close. She remembered how she and her brothers used to watch him from the barn through the telescopic sights of the hunting rifle, and sometimes aimed just above his head at the tin roof of his house or hit one of his animals. She, too, sometimes crept to the barn and watched him through the sights; he had a better figure than her brothers, was almost always clean-shaven, and when he was wearing his denim overalls and a flannel shirt he reminded her, with his broad face and strong teeth, of the man from a TV commercial for blue jeans, and sometimes she felt a gentle shiver in her body, and her hand slid down her body and stopped in the soft, warm bush below her belly. She didn't know whether it was right, she often felt disgusted at herself afterward, she hated the man across the boundary line, she hated him because she had to hate him, everybody in her family hated him, and yet it sometimes seemed that when she looked at him her already warm bush was set on fire, and she couldn't, didn't want to resist the sensation. Sometimes she took her sewing and knitting up to the barn, and then she kept looking over there toward him, watching him working in the field, feeding his animals and throwing his wild dogs chunks of bloody meat. She also occasionally saw him spread a piece of canvas between wooden poles and paint for hours and hours. It seemed ridiculous to her, nobody in her house ever did anything like that; through the rifle sights she watched the colors on the canvas and felt good inside. "It's pretty," the thought rushed though her mind. "It's funny, what this man is doing," she whispered to herself. It sometimes happened that one of her brothers noticed that the neighbor had forgotten to hide the canvas drying behind the house, and he pierced the painting with lead bullets. She always laughed at that, she carried in her veins the hatred toward the handsome neighbor who was making their life bitter, she openly hated and covertly admired him for daring to resist them all by himself; sometimes, feeling enraged at him, when he perforated their milk canisters, when he beat up one of the brothers down in the valley, or when his dogs slaughtered one of their animals, she was thinking how she would like to scratch the skin on his clean-shaven, pretty face with her nails, and she shivered with a deep, sensuous desire to do just that.

She put her father into the bed, covered his fat, old body and crept out of the house.

He felt a wet tingling sensation on his face, opened his eyes, and through the aching swellings saw his St. Bernard licking his face. The morning sun was shining, mist was rising from the ground in pale, milky waves. With difficulty he moved his head, looked around, he couldn't remember what had happened, then it dawned on him. "The neighbors," he sighed. His entire body ached, he moved his hand, it slid along thick shaggy cloth, he looked down at his body. During the night somebody had covered him with a blanket, he didn't dwell on the thought who that might have been—he didn't know anybody who'd do that for him. He grabbed the dog 'round the neck and sat up, felt a piercing pain in his ribs, coughed and spat out some clotted blood. On the road he saw a heap of metal and the remains of car tires. "There would have been nothing left of me," he mumbled, "perhaps a tooth on the gravel, a button among the bushes along the road." His body was nothing but a mass of pain, yet he stood up, picked up a dry stick from the grass and staggered down the road. His legs were shaking; after a few steps he stopped in front of the logs lying across the road, leaned onto the stick and tried to lift his leg high, but couldn't; he lurched, fell over across the logs and hit the wood hard with his shoulder. He remained lying on his back and stared into the clear sky; he was familiar with the feeling of helplessness; once, when he was skiing in the mountains, he was swept away in an avalanche and buried underneath it, and although in his mind had given up, after a few minutes he felt such a strong desire to live that he couldn't resist it, and against his own intentions, he dug himself out from under the snow and dragged himself down to the valley with a broken leg. The sun was hurting his eyes, after a while he propped his feet against the logs, rolled over onto his belly, rolled to the other side of the pile of lumber and stood up. "This is not the end yet," he mumbled, "not the end yet." And barely managing to stay upright, he stumbled toward his home only a couple of hundred yards away.

When he unlocked the chain and walked through the large screech-ing gate of his property, his pack of dogs came bounding toward him. He stood there, leaning against the fence; they jumped up to him, knocked him over, licked his clotted blood and snarled. "They'll attack me," he thought. "They'll fight for their master, tear him apart in their blind bloody beastly love." He wasn't afraid, through the slits of his swollen lids he watched their bloodshot, hungry, devoted eyes, the drizzle of their saliva, the glittering of their fur in the morning sun. He called out their names and touched their sharp teeth with his hand. "In this world the only loyal creatures are the animals," he thought in his aching and dizzy head, then he whistled sharply; the dogs bounded toward the house and sat down on the steps. He pulled himself up and staggered as far as the house, went in, took a couple of chunks of raw meat from the fridge and threw them out. He had no more strength to go to the bathroom to look at his beaten face; he dragged himself to his bed and immedi-ately went to sleep.

In the afternoon he was awoken by a fierce barking, he got up quickly and whimpered with pain, slithered to the window and heard shooting. He knew where it was coming from; he grabbed his rifle and opened the window. The brothers were standing in the small wood behind his fence and the electric wire, shooting at his dogs, he could see two of the dogs lying motionless on the ground, he lifted his rifle and started shooting at the neighbors. Never before had he aimed straight at them, but now he didn't care what would happen if he killed them. He heard them shout-ing, one of them was yelling and rolling on the ground. He knew he'd hit one, he was aiming at the man lying on the ground, he was a sitting duck, he cocked the trigger and then paused for an instant. He felt hatred inside himself, breathed the air in through his nostrils, his strained ribs hurt, he felt like porcelain just before it breaks. He fired into the air, into the treetops, none of the brothers dared approach the one who was wounded and sobbing and holding his shoulder.

Silence filled with suspense hung above the landscape, he watched the young woman running from the neighboring property toward the boundary line; he knew she was the sister, he'd met her down in the village two or three times when she came shopping with her brothers. She had a nice figure, large breasts; in the old days, when he was just over twenty, he had found pleasure with that kind of woman. It was all in the past; he hadn't had a woman for years, and didn't even miss one. "That would be fine revenge," he thought and watched the woman, aiming at her with the gun, he heard the brothers screaming, they wanted to stop her from getting to the one who was wounded, but she ran to him all the same and leaned over him, his hands were shaking, he closed his eyes and imagined pulling the trigger, he imagined the flight of the bullet through the warm spring air and a tiny dribble of blood on the young woman's forehead. No, he couldn't shoot her, he opened his eyes and saw the girl dragging her brother toward the wood, he became aware of his two dead dogs in the field, sent another bullet into the air and went back to bed.

They dragged the wounded brother to the house; he was moaning and breathing deeply.

"Somebody shot him in the shoulder," the oldest brother said to the father, who was sitting in the wheelchair in front of the front door.

"And what did you do to him?" asked the old man.

"Nothing," the oldest replied. "We were out in the open, and he was hiding in the house." The old man swung his stick toward him, but he couldn't reach him.

"Idiots! Who do you think it was, eh?" he hissed at his sons with a voice that ended in a rattling whisper.

"It wasn't him," somebody said. "Yesterday he burned to death in his car."

"We soaked him in gas and set him alight," somebody said.

"I went to check today," somebody said. "There was nothing left, just a heap of metal."

"We beat him to death and burned him," somebody said. "We all saw he was dead."

"Yesterday you said you didn't kill him," the old man groaned.

"We killed him, Father," said the oldest.

"We killed him," somebody else repeated.

"You didn't kill him," the old man said quietly, ominously. "Now it'll start all over again." From under the blanket covering his legs, he pulled out a handgun, raised his shaking hand and shot in the direction of the neighbor's property until he ran out of bullets.

They carried the wounded brother into the house. Klara watched the brothers trying to take the bullet out of his shoulder. She thought of the neighbor; she was sorry she'd covered him with a blanket during the night. "I should've told them I found him alive in the ditch," she thought, but didn't dare speak up.

"We'll have to take him down to the valley," the oldest said.

"What will we say?" somebody asked.

"Nothing," said the oldest. "A hunting accident."

"We'll get our own back," somebody said.

"Yes, we'll get our own back," somebody said.

"This time we'll kill him," somebody said.

"We've killed him already," somebody said.

"No, we didn't kill him," somebody said. "It was him in the house, the old man's right. Who else could it be?"

"We'll wait a few days, then we'll burn his house," somebody said.

"Yes," the oldest said, "now it's gone too far. We'll do that."

They put the brother into the van and took him down to the valley. The father gazed sharply after them, he was holding a cigarette between his lips, his face was yellow from nicotine, it had been a long time since he last held a cigarette with his hands, he'd light one and hold it between his lips, the ashes dropping onto his jacket and blanket, nicotine saliva dribbling from the corners of his mouth. He didn't feel sorry for his wounded son; for him, the children were like his livestock, part of his estate, part of his property. "I did everything myself," he gurgled to himself. "I bought everything myself, they're only waiting for me to croak. But I won't do them that favor, I'll survive them," he said stubbornly. "I'll survive them all." His head dropped onto his chest, his daughter watched him with a mixture of fear and pity; she stepped closer and took the smoldering butt out of his mouth. He wasn't asleep, he knew it was her. "Klara is all I've got," he thought to himself, tears gathering under his closed lids. "I'll sell the land and leave the money to her," he murmured and a tear slid down his cheek. "She should find a man down in the valley, someone like what I used to be," he sobbed. He was sobbing in a screechy, stifling voice, his wife came out of the house and asked what was wrong; without looking up he threw his stick at her and kept sobbing inconsolably.

In the evening the brothers returned without the one who had been wounded; he'd been kept at the hospital. Over dinner the father stared at them gloomily, nobody dared speak up. He was downing one glass of brandy after another, his bloodshot eyes staring vacantly from his dead-pale face. The space before his eyes was dissolving; everything was a heavy undulation of air with pieces of furniture and indiscernible faces floating through it. He made a circling motion above his head with one hand; he wanted to brush away the images he was seeing, the mass of dissolved, interchanging faces. Their silence was driving him crazy; he thought he was yelling at them and they didn't talk back, yet in fact he was silent, only in his head everything was confused, the past and the present, illusion and reality, shapes and emptiness. "I'm going to Australia tomorrow," he finally gurgled drunkenly, belched and pushed himself away from the table; the chair hurtled to the wall, the metal hit the wood with a loud noise, and his head jerked down onto his chest as he hit the shelf. He felt the swarming of a narrow sharp pain in the temple, as if somebody was threading a needle through his head; he felt the moist wet pain under the scalp, it seemed to him that his brain and eyes were being filled with blood.

In the morning he didn't wake up. They left him in bed until midday, and when his wife tried to put him in the chair she realized he was dead. She went to the kitchen and told the others. They were silent, staring at her vacantly; only the daughter had tears in her eyes.

"Did he tell you?" the oldest finally asked.

"What?" asked the mother.

"Where he'd buried the gold."

She looked at the empty, tense, hostile faces of her sons. No, he didn't tell her.

"He told me. When you get rid of the neighbor, I'll show you," she said quietly and stubbornly.

"Yes, he's responsible for the old man's death," said the oldest.

"Yes," somebody said, "now we have no choice."

"Yes," somebody said, "we must kill him."

"I'll kill him," somebody said.

"No, we'll kill him together," said the oldest.

"Yes, you have to do it together," said the mother. "You have to do it for your father." They buried their father the following day. It was pouring rain, and the roads were flooded with dirty brown streams.

"Now you'll listen to me," said the oldest brother, when they got home covered in mud.

"No, until you get rid of the neighbor and dig up the gold you'll listen to me," said the mother.

"Yes, we'll listen to her," somebody else said.

"He's right, we'll listen to her," said the others.

In the following days, one of the brothers continually watched the neighbor's house through the rifle sights. For the first few days he couldn't be seen; they assumed that he'd gone down to the valley, that he'd fled, but they didn't dare cross over to his property, they only shot at his dogs from a distance. Then one day he emerged in front of the house, walked about all bent over, he was quite feeble, he'd spent more than a week in bed; just once a day he threw some food to the dogs through the window and in the evening milked the cows so that their udders wouldn't burst. His face was covered in blue-green bruises, his ribs still hurt, and day-light irritated his eyes. "I should go down to the valley for food," he thought, but he had no car and was too weak to ride his horse. He knew the neighbors were watching him, he felt their hostile, dim eyes on his body; he wasn't afraid, he just felt sorry that he couldn't live differently. He couldn't leave the property of his parents, and although he some-times considered selling it all and moving away, he didn't want to do it, he was too attached to his property in the embrace of the mountains, to the silent graves of his parents at the forest edge, to the freedom restricted by the violence of the neighbors. After all that had happened he couldn't give up, he was sure the brothers were responsible for his father's death; he was taking his revenge by not giving in. A bullet hit the metal part of his house, he wasn't upset, he knew they were only challenging him, they didn't dare kill him just like that, they'd once more try to stage a dirty little accident like a fire or a fall off his horse. He put some lime in a bucket and slowly walked toward the forest dividing the two properties; the two dead dogs were decaying under their fur and giving off a putrid stench, a swarm of insects were circling above them; he sprinkled them with lime and said their names into their deaf, decay-ing, hairy ears.

She was watching him through the rifle sights, his broad face was sunken, the skin between his strong cheeks and the chin was sagging, his shoulders were stooping. He was sprinkling the lime powder onto the dogs like a gardener sowing seeds into the ground, she felt something warm while watching him, now she was no longer sorry she'd gone and covered him up that night. For the first time since her father's death she thought she'd definitely leave her home one day, this world suddenly wasn't her world any more, her brothers had started fighting among themselves, they were drinking almost every night and the mother could hardly restrain them. It also seemed to her that the oldest brother had started stalking her as he would a woman, and she felt sick at the thought that he could actually do something to her; she'd kill herself first, she'd kill him first.

During the night she put some bread, cheese, and noodles into a black plastic bag and took it secretly to the neighbor's fence. He heard the barking of his dogs, took his gun, and went to the window. The dogs kept barking fiercely for a while, then they went quiet. He stared fixedly into the night, checked that the switch for the wired fence was on, turned on the flashlight and with it scanned the property; there was nothing unusual to be seen, so he went back to bed and took the gun with him.

In the morning he saw the torn-up black plastic bag by the fence. "They've thrown down poison again," he thought. He looked around his property, but none of his dogs were distorted with pain, they came running toward him as usual with their tails up. He walked to the bag and with the tip of his shoe poked out the noodles, cheese, and remains of the bread, picked the things up and took them into the house. He didn't know what it meant. "They won't get me so easily," he said and threw the food into the garbage.

The following night, at more or less the same time, he again heard barking, took his gun and crept to the fence, but there was nobody there; only a black bag filled with food was lying on the ground. He dragged it into the house and left it in the hallway.

"Somebody went out at night," the oldest brother said in the morning when they started off toward the forest.

"It wasn't me," somebody said.

"Me neither," somebody said.

"It wasn't any of us," somebody said.

"Who was it then?" asked the oldest.

"We don't know," somebody said.

The following day he was strong enough to run the tractor to the field; suspense hung in the air as if before a storm, the birds were flying low and the livestock kept to the shed. He knew he was being watched; his pistol was in his pocket. He wasn't afraid of them, he wasn't afraid of anybody, he'd come to terms with the fact that he could be shot down any instant, but he didn't want to live in fear, it was too late to give up. He had barely started working when the air trembled with a muffled thunder, it seemed as if the mountains would collapse and bury him, it started to pour rain, but stopped minutes later just as suddenly as it had started. He worked in the field till evening, his body still ached, but he felt he had gotten out of it well, his body was strong, used to hardship and blows, it was stronger than his own will.

At night he took the gun, switched off the current in the wiring and crept to the fence. He slid through the wires and hid in the forest. The neighbors' house was dark; he looked intently into the motionless night for almost an hour. He was about to leave when he noticed somebody coming down the hill of the neighboring property. He took cover and watched the gentle silent steps of the young woman. She came near his fence, the dogs started barking, she threw the bag across and turned around. He dropped the gun and blocked her way. She was frightened and wanted to run away, but he took hold of her arm. She screamed and tried to break free. He didn't let go, he put his arm round her waist, she resisted, grabbed him by the neck and they both fell over. He felt a piercing pain in the ribs, they rolled in the leaves, her firm, soft body was strong, he could hardly restrain her; with his fingers he held her hands down, pressed her to the ground with his aching chest and pressed her legs as in a vise with his own. She was breathing deeply, her deep eyes stared fixedly into his, her wet lips glistened in the moonlight, her soft breasts made him soft. She was panting wildly and submissively, she closed her eyes, let her head drop back and pushed part of her tongue out of her mouth. He slowly lowered his mouth toward hers and touched her tongue with his lips. With tiny crackling kisses he went across her face, she was soft and willing, she was giving her warm body to him, she loved and hated the man on top of her, she didn't want to resist him; with sharp, muffled sighs she interrupted the silence as he was undressing her. The dogs by the fence were barking fiercely at their close struggle, at her panting, sweat gathering on their skin in the meager light of the moon.

First one shot cut though the warm spring night, and then there were explosions on all sides. The trees suddenly trembled violently, the air filled with the thick whirling murmur of leaves, the smell of decaying animals and rotten roots arose from the soil, the stars dissolved into huge melting yellow carpets. He was sliding down a funnel of white light that was sucking in his body. He felt her strong embrace, he saw a smile on her lips, the twitching thin cord of life hummed in the air; they remained motionless in a puddle of blood.

Translated by LILI POTPARA

About the Contributors

THE EDITORS

Editor **Mitja Čander** was born in Maribor, Slovenia. He studied comparative literature at the Faculty of Art, Ljubljana University. From 1995 to 2000 he was the editor of the literary supplement of the Maribor literary magazine, *Dialogi*. Since 1996, he has been editor of Slovenia's leading literary press, Beletrina, an imprint of Študentska založba Academic Press in Ljubljana. Čander has received two major awards: the Stritar Award (1998) for the best young critic, and the Glazer Prize (2000), awarded by the city of Maribor, for his cultural contributions to the city.

Coeditor **Tom Priestly** was born in Kampala, Uganda, and currently lives in Canada, where he has resided since 1966. A graduate of Downing College, Cambridge, he received his PhD from Simon Fraser University, B.C., in 1970. In 1992 he retired from more than twenty-two years teaching Russian and Slavic Linguistics at the University of Alberta. He is fluent in Russian, German, French, and Slovene, and is the author, coauthor, or translator of dozens of books and articles.

THE WRITERS

Andrej Blatnik is one of the most widely translated contemporary Slovene writers, with his short stories and novels published in more than ten languages. In addition to his own collection *Skinswaps* (1998), his works in English are included in the 1994 anthology *The Day Tito Died: Contemporary Slovenian Stories*, edited by Drago Jančar. Born in 1963 in Ljubljana, Blatnik currently works as the editor at the Cankarjeva založba.

Aleš Čar was born in 1971 in Idrija, Slovenia. He studied comparative literature at the Faculty of Arts and Sciences in Ljubljana. A writer, publicist, translator, and screenwriter, Čar has published two novels—*When Bats Dance with Angels* (1997) and *Dog Tango* (1999)—and a collection of short prose—*Out of Order* (2003).

Dušan Čater was born in 1968 in Celje, Slovenia. After graduating from secondary school, he studied sociology at the Faculty for Social Sciences in Ljubljana. He has been the editor at the publishing house Karantanija and has published three novels—*Imitation* (1995), *Pathos* (1999), *Father Is Drunk Again* (2002)—and two collections of short prose—*Flash Royal* (1994) and *True Murders* (1997).

Polona Glavan, born in 1974, is youngest author in this anthology. She graduated in comparative literature and English from the Faculty of Arts and Sciences in Ljubljana. She has published one novel, *A Night in Europe* (2002), and is a translator of literature and theoretical writings from English.

Mohor Hudej was born in 1968 in Celje, Slovenia. After graduating from secondary school, he studied comparative literature at the Faculty of Arts and Sciences in Ljubljana. He currently works as a librarian in Celje. He has published a collection of short prose, *Mumps at a Ripe Age* (1995).

Tomaž Kosmač was born in 1965 in Godovič, Slovenia. He is a freelance writer and has published two collections of short prose—*Diarrhea* (1998) and *Sad but True* (2001).

Mojca Kumerdej is a philosopher, a cultural chronicler, a theater critic, and the author of the short story collection *Fragma* (2003) and the novel *The Baptism over Mount Triglav* (2001), which is a parody of one of the most important literary works in Slovenian literary history, France Prešeren's 1835 epic poem "The Baptism at the Savica."

Miha Mazzini's *The Cartier Project* is one of Slovenia all-time best-selling novels, with more than 50,000 copies sold at the time of its publication in 1987. Published in the United States in 2004, *The Cartier Project* was named a "Top 10 Novel" of 2005 by the *Detroit Free Press*. Mazzini's novel *Guarding Hanna* is forthcoming as part of North Atlantic Books' Scala Translation Series.

Andrej Morovič was born in 1960 in Ljubljana. After graduating from secondary school in Koper, he traveled abroad, earning his living as a day laborer. He has published three novels—*Bomba la Petrolia* (1989), *Tekavec* (1993), and *The Ruler* (1997)—and four collections of short prose—*Opportunities in the Street* (1985), *Freewheeling* (1986), *Parachutists* (1992), and *Divers* (1992).

Maja Novak was born in 1960 in Jesenice, Slovenia. She holds a law degree from the Law Faculty in Ljubljana and has received several prizes for her work. Her books have been translated into several languages. She has published four novels—*Behind the Congress or Murder in Territorial Waters* (1993), *Roommates* (1995), *Karfanaum* (1998), and *The Feline Plague* (2000), which is forthcoming as part of North Atlantic Books' Scala Translation Series.

Andrej E. Skubič was born in 1967 and has been publishing prose in Slovenian literary reviews since 1989. He has translated several English works into Slovenian, including *Trainspotting* by Irvine Welsh and *The Butcher Boy* by Patrick McCabe. His 1999 novel *Bitter Honey* received the Kresnik Novel of the Year Award and the Debut of the Year Award. His second novel, *Fužine Blues* (2001), was nominated for the Kresnik Award and was adapted for the stage by the Slovenian National Theater.

The Slovenian poet **Aleš Šteger** (coauthor of the introduction) was born in 1973 in Ptuj, Slovenia. He studied comparative literature and German at the University of Ljubljana. He has published three volumes of poetry —*Chess Desks of Hours* (1995), *Kashmere* (1997), and *Protuberances* (2002). His books have been translated into several languages.

Suzana Tratnik was born in 1963 in Murska Sobota, Slovenia. She holds a Master's Degree in gender anthropology from Ljubljana Graduate School of Humanities. She is credited with organizing the first lesbian organization in Slovenia—LL (Lesbian Lilit)—in 1987. Her short stories have been published in several Slovenian literary and cultural magazines and have been included in *The Vintage Book of International Lesbian Fiction* (1999). She is the author of the short story collections *Below Zero* (1998) and *In One's Own Backyard* (2003) and the novel, *My Name Is Damian* (2001).

Jani Virk was born in 1962 in Ljubljana. He graduated with a degree in German and comparative literature from the Faculty of Arts and Sciences in Ljubljana. He was the chief editor of the magazine *Literatura* (1988–1989), the culture editor and the chief editor of the daily *Slovenec,* and the culture editor for national television. Currently he is the editor of the culture-documentary program for national television. His novels include *Rachel* (1998), *The Earthquake of 1895* (1995), *The Last Temptation of Sergej* (1996), and *Laughter behind the Wooden Partition* (2000).

ABOUT THE TRANSLATORS

Erica Johnson Debeljak is an American-born writer and translator. Her stories have appeared recently in *Prairie Schooner, Missouri Review,* and *Epoch* and will soon be published in *Glimmer Train.* Her memoir is forthcoming from North Atlantic Books.

Kelly Lenox's recent translations are included in *Chasms* (2003), a chapbook of translations of the Slovene poet Barbara Korun; *Voice in the Body* (2005); and *Six Slovenian Poets* (2006). She currently lives in Portland, Oregon.

David Limon holds a doctorate in linguistics and teaches at the Department of Translation, University of Ljubljana. Eight of his translations appear in the anthology *A Sunny Sunday Afternoon* (2007). His translation of Andrej Skubič's prize-winning novel *Fužine Blues* recently appeared as part of the *Litterae Slovenicae* series (2007).

Maja Visenjak Limon has a degree in English language and literature and comparative literature. She has translated three novels by Miha Mazzini (*Guarding Hanna* [2002]; *The Cartier Project* [2004]; and *The King of the Rattling Spirits* [2004]). She is currently translating Maja Novak's novel *The Feline Plague*, to be published in North Atlantic Books' Scala Translation Series.

Tom Lozar has written for several Canadian newspapers and magazines and publishes regularly in Slovenian publications. For the past five years, he has written a column in the Maribor daily, *Večer*. He is the translator of a collection by the Slovenian poet Edvard Kocbek, *At the Door at Evening* (1990), and of a poem he considers one of the greatest of the twentieth century, Gregor Strniša's "There Was a Tiger Here."

Lili Potpara's translations include the prize-winning collection of essays *Notes from the Night* by Mitja Čander (2003), the novella *When the Birches Up There Are Greening* by Breda Smolnikar (2005), and several stories from Drago Jančar's *Joyce's Pupil* (2006). Her collection of short stories, *Bottoms-Up Stories*, won the Best Literary Debut prize in Slovenia in 2002, and her second book of short prose, *Please, Read It*, was published in 2006.

Tamara M. Soban received her BA in English from the University of Ljubljana. Her translations include Andrej Blatnik's collection of short stories, *Skinswaps* (1998), and Feri Lainšček's novel, *For Whom Does the Flower Bloom* (2002). For the past four years, she has worked for the Museum of Modern Art in Ljubljana as a translator and editor.

Laura Cuder Turk was born in Ljubljana and graduated from the University of Ljubljana with degrees in English and sociology. She currently lives in Suhadole, Slovenia, with her husband, son, and daughter.

Elizabeta Žargi was born and raised in Montreal, Canada. After completing her studies at McGill University, she moved to Ljubljana, Slovenia, where she teaches ESL and translates. She recently cotranslated the collection of poetry *What He Ought to Know* by the American poet Edward Foster (2007).

The Scala Translation Series

Angels Beneath the Surface is published as part of a partnership between North Atlantic Books and Scala House Press.

The mission of the Scala Translation Series is to publish fiction and literary nonfiction to help develop and foster connections between writers from diverse international cultures and their English-speaking readers around the world. Memoirs, occasional poetry anthologies, and works of literature in this series all seek to explore the qualities that bind and define the human community, while celebrating distinctive traditions and tastes. We are looking for new and original voices, as well as celebrated or neglected works to introduce to English-speaking readers. We are particularly supportive of women's voices. Our publishing goals rest on the premise that good literature, like all good art, has the potential to undermine sectarianism, ideologies, and boundaries that divide us within and outside of national boundaries.

The works we support and celebrate capture the political, historical, personal, or spiritual currents of particular eras and times, drawing out the subtleties of the individual struggle for identity and grace deep within these defining moments.

Other Books in the Scala Translation Series

Alamut
A novel by Vladimir Bartol, translated from Slovenian by Michael Biggins.
$16.95, ISBN 978-1-55643-681-9, 400 pages. (November 2007)

Guarding Hanna
A novel by Miha Mazzini, translated from Slovenian by Maja Visenjak-Limon.
$15.95, ISBN 978-1-55643-726-7, 272 pages. (June 2008)

Belonging: New Poetry by Iranians Around the World
Edited by Niloufar Talebi.
$18.95, ISBN 978-1-55643-712-0, 256 pages. (July 2008)

Bringing Tony Home
A novella and stories by Tissa Abeysekara.
$14.95, ISBN 978-1-55643-757-1, 224 pages. (November 2008)